A Pilgrim Stranger

Ulymas Press

A Pilgrim Stranger

Stranger

Mark Samuels

A PILGRIM STRANGER

Copyright © 2017 Mark Samuels

First paperback edition, 2017
2nd Corrected printing

Ulymas Press

PREFACE

I completed the first draft of this novel in April 2016 and, aside from the usual editorial revision, have not altered the text in light of the subsequent political events on both sides of the Atlantic. It is perilous to claim a work of fiction can ever be prophetic; and I do not do so in this instance. It is only as a satire on certain aspects of modernity, as an expression of religious faith, and on its own aesthetic merits that I hope A PILGRIM STRANGER will ultimately be judged.

Mark Samuels, January 2017.

CHAPTER ONE

DENNIS Spencer, history teacher at the Southwood Secondary Comprehensive School for Boys, threw his broken wristwatch into the open fire in the staff-room. He saw its glass front turn black and then shatter, while its brown leather band curled up in the flames. Cheap rubbish from the market.

Then he wandered over to the mirror in the staff-room and ran a narrow comb through his Trotsky beard. After several attempts he succeeded in subjugating the dissident strands of hair and finally lit the B&H cigarette that dangled from the corner of his mouth.

Last night had been a real triumph. All of the teachers had got together straight after school in the Woodman pub and drank heavily from four p.m. until closing time. Somehow he had wound up with the French supply teacher, a young woman called Marie,

1

and found himself waking up in her bed-sit after a night of strenuous and multiple exchanges of bodily fluids.

There was something of an awkward scene in the morning over the Wheetabix and coffee, but Spencer didn't allow himself to dwell upon it. He knew that half the male staff had been riding that Gallic bicycle this term. He was, after all, very much in favour of women's rights. A liberated woman, should, like a liberated man, walk away from a night of hot drunken passion with the absolute equality of both parties intact. Still, the momentary thing about lack of rubbers had been awkward, but he'd persuaded her that he'd withdraw at the climax.

His hangover, he calculated, should have receded sometime after three. Around the correct hour to enjoy the first round at the pub this afternoon.

Spencer had no love of teaching and had drifted into it by accident. He had thought, after leaving Manchester University, to try his hand at writing historical books. He'd even spent a year on and off working on his *Magnum Opus* about the Independent Labour Party during the 1930s, but when he realised he was saying nothing radically new, he gave it up.

Though there were drawbacks to teaching history, nevertheless, it was pretty satisfactory for a man in his mid-twenties. Six weeks off in the summer, augmented by N.U.T. strikes throughout the year, only working from nine until three thirty, and, most of all, not being contradicted, well, it was good enough for any young socialist.

He stubbed out the B&H and made himself a brew, opening a fresh bottle of milk by jabbing a finger directly into the gold foil at the top. He sniffed at the liquid. The cream at the top would curdle the rest. Rather like Maggie Thatcher, the milk-snatcher, now two years into her Downing Street dictatorship.

The old teapot was black inside and tiny flakes of residue came away from the bowl and seeped into the boiling water from the electric kettle.

He sat down in the nearest armchair, under the framed photo of a pipe-puffing Tony Benn the staff had hung on the wall to annoy the Headmaster, put the mug of tea on the floor, went through his battered soft leather briefcase and drew out his notes for this morning's classes. First up was Queen Elizabeth the First and the Spanish Armada with 3A. Nothing too taxing. He knew the subject so well he could give the class almost entirely from memory. Class 3A was the top stream for the third year, about twenty-five boys. One or two were bright. He doubted if any of them would eventually get a higher grade than "C" in their O Level exams on the subject though. Still, "C" was a pass so there was something to be said for it. Spencer felt he had scored a major victory by persuading the brightest of the bunch to read *The Guardian* newspaper a few times a week. It wasn't long before they began to paraphrase its political views as if they had arrived at them independently. The next stage was to get them onto *The Morning Star*, but that often proved contentious, especially if parents found out, and so had to be handled more carefully. Still, someone had to provide a corrective to the threat of the skinhead National Front brigade who hung around outside the school gates shouting about "red traitors" and trying to sell kids copies of *Bulldog*.

Some of the other teachers had drifted into the staffroom and were either smoking or drinking tea in glum silence. He nodded at Alan Vickery who winked and then smirked, obviously in honour to Spencer's night before with the French supply teacher. He had done the same thing, only a week previously. But the rest of them were a lifeless lot, half-dead on school premises unless on an N.U.T. picket line blocking the entrance.

Wednesday mornings were always the worst. Smack bang in the middle of the week, exactly half-way across the great desert of Monday to Friday. Looking over the top of his notes Spencer saw old Mr. Browne (a dead-ringer for the telly personality, poet laureate and old duffer Sir John Betjeman) his bald pate bright red and aureoled by white hair, surreptitiously top up his mug of tea with a generous clout of whisky from a hip flask. His hands were trembling with feverish excitement. Perhaps it was as a result of D.T.s, or the thought of slippering the boys in his class. Spencer took a sense of progressive pride in the fact he hadn't resorted to using his own green plimsoll for the last four terms. In fact, he was often vocal on the subject of all corporal punishment being banned, despite opposition from the Tory Head and Deputy Head Masters.

The warning bell rang and Spencer slipped into the armour of his ink-stained tweed jacket. One by one the teachers scuttled out of the staff-room, some adjusting their ties and others swearing under their breath. By the second time the bell rang the hallways were empty and the school began its process of the daily education of malleable young minds.

Ж

Spencer had forgotten that a new boy was due to start school today. The headmaster, Mr. Hargreaves, had informed him a week ago, but it was only when he went through the register, before class, that he noticed the new, unfamiliar name; Alfredo Salgado. When the boys filed in Salgado took up a seat at the desk right at the front of the class and sat staring with a strange expression in his eyes that was a combination of vacancy and intent. Rather like those of a hungry fish, in a glass tank, that knows it is about to be fed something.

The name, Spencer supposed, indicated that the boy was Spanish or Latin American, but when he called the register Salgado's reply was in an accent as English as any London boy's. He was certainly an odd-looking creature though. Nothing wrong with his uniform, which was spotless, his shoes shined to gleaming perfection, and his tie very neat and properly done up. His jet-black hair, however, was like a brush, sticking straight up on the top of his head and closely shaved around the sides. And his face was, without being in any sense deformed, nevertheless reminiscent somehow of a pug dog, being all crumpled up around a squat nose. He wore a pair of N.H.S. standard issue glasses, with black plastic rims, behind which stared the unblinking fish-eyes Spencer had first noted.

He thought of asking the boy to change his seat with someone else, and move towards the middle or back of the classroom, for having this entity right in front of him for the whole lesson was something of a distraction, but Spencer decided not to do so. The boy was new and he didn't want to take the chance of being seen to take against him in front of the rest of the class, especially not on his first day. Salgado had probably already come in for a fair share of the usual distrust a newcomer experiences when thrown into the society of fellow schoolboys.

Anyway, Spencer thought, he could take this lesson in his sleep. He pulled out his own copy of the school textbook on the history of the Tudor monarchs and asked the rest of them to take out their copies from their desks. The boys complied, noisily, and he handed out a spare copy to Salgado who proceeded to desultorily leaf through it.

Spencer had been explaining the causes behind the failed attempted invasion of England by the Spanish Armada for several minutes, in a kind of comforting trance. He had been wandering around the classroom benevolently, when he finally noticed that the boy Salgado had been playing with something between his fingers the whole time and not paying attention.

Now that he had stopped talking Spencer heard the faint sound of beads rattling and a low murmuring coming from Salgado.

He came down the aisle of desks, bent over the boy and snatched the thing from his grasp.

"What's this?" said Spencer.

"It is a rosary, Sir," Salgado replied.

A few of the wags who sat at the back of the class giggled loudly.

"I know that," Spencer said. "What are you doing with it?"

"Praying."

"Look, you shouldn't be praying in class, you should be paying attention to the lesson."

Spencer put the rosary in the right pocket of his tweed coat.

"You can have it back when the class is over," Spencer said.

Salgado was staring him quite impertinently.

"*Pirata*," the boy said, under his breath.

"What the bloody hell do you mean by that?" Spencer said, his voice raised.

"In your analysis of the historical situation you made no mention of certain *casus belli*. Firstly, the illegitimate Queen's patronage of English pirate raids upon Spanish galleons carrying gold back from the New World," replied the boy, who was still glaring at him fixedly and offensively.

The wags were beginning to find this scene highly entertaining and a few of the other, usually more timid, pupils, also began to giggle.

Well, the Salgado boy was clever, thought Spencer, and certainly had a way with words, but this had to be quashed right away. He was about to reply when Salgado launched another salvo.

"In addition, you ignore the fact that Felipe II of

Spain was also the legitimate King of England and had reigned jointly with Queen Mary Tudor. You take no account of the truth that the Catholic Faithful numbered half of the populace of England."

"Eh, what's that? Bloody Mary? Burning alive heretics, eh?" Spencer said, his voice reaching a decibel level that silenced the rest of the class at once. Though it did nothing to lessen the obvious pleasure they derived from the spectacle and the distraction it provided from the usual tedious history lesson given by Spencer.

But Salgado was not cowed in the slightest. His fishy eyes narrowed and he carried on as if addressing a particularly backward younger pupil, and not his own teacher.

"To continue. Lastly, you are obviously ignorant of, or choose to disregard, I know not which, the prior attacks by English pirates, led by the perfidious Dragon, whom you call Sir Francis Drake, who, with the English fleet in 1587 raided up and down the Spanish coast, in an act of clear provocation."

"I am sorry," Spencer shouted, holding up the textbook. "If the recommended standard textbook for the modern history curriculum in English schools, *The Condensed History of the Tudors* is not good enough for you. Perhaps you should write to its author, Professor Harold Raker-Stroker, of Christ Church College, Oxford and draw his attention to his omissions! I am sure he would be glad to receive correction from a schoolboy!"

Spencer took a deep breath.

Quite well done, he thought, two can play at this game of verbal verbosity.

"I imagine such a correspondence would be one-sided, Sir. Professor Raker-Stroker died in 1976," Salgado replied calmly.

The class descended into chaos. Desk tops were slammed up and down, torn pieces of paper thrown into the air and the boys started cheering wildly. It took Spencer five minutes to regain order. He told Salgado to go outside and wait in the corridor until the class was over and then to come back inside afterwards.

As he made his way out, the boy stopped and asked for his rosary.

"I hope you will have no objection to my praying in the corridor while I wait, Sir," he said.

Spencer handed the thing over.

Ж

The farce of a lesson was over, the pupils had all filed out, and Spencer sat his desk mulling over his thoughts. Finally, though, he called Salgado back in, who was still in the corridor and presumably rattling his beads.

The boy was obviously highly intelligent and his vocabulary was remarkable. It was very obvious to

Spencer that he was the product of some kind of Roman Catholic nutcase family, probably ultramontane. Quite how or why the boy had ended up in this state school, where the only sop to religion was a mumbled ten second prayer given by the Headmaster at assembly in the main hall and the amorphous hodge-podge of comparative religion provided in the R.E. classes once a week, Spencer could not understand. Had his objection to Queen Elizabeth the First and all the rest of it been a question of supporting republicanism over monarchy, i.e. progress over tradition, Spencer would have encouraged him in front of the other boys, but it was obvious it was nothing of the sort. Well, something would have to be done.

He opened the door to the classroom and peered along the corridor. Salgado was leaning against the wooden lockers and peering at the crucifix on his rosary.

"Come in here, Salgado," Spencer said.

The boy strode in, his back bolt straight, his head erect, fearless.

Spencer sat down behind his desk, keeping Salgado standing in front of it. For a moment he considered slippering him but he suspected that the boy would probably regard it as some form of welcome martyrdom.

"You're obviously clever for your age. But I cannot

tolerate this sort of behaviour in a lesson," the teacher said. "If you have any questions about what's being taught, you raise your hand. If I do not ask you for your opinion, you do not give your opinion. This is not a debating hall, it is where you are here to learn and I am here to teach, *my* classroom. Are we clear?"

"*Ne terreàmini ab his, qui vos persequúntur,*" Salgado said.

"This is London, not Madrid. You will speak in English, not Spanish," Spencer replied.

"I'm afraid it's Latin, Sir," said Salgado. "Saint Luke chapter twelve, verse four."

Spencer ground his teeth together audibly. He felt he was left with no other option, but the very last resort, in order to exert his authority. He opened the top drawer of his desk and drew out the dreaded green plimsoll.

"Bend over the desk," he said, rolling up his sleeves.

Ж

It was lunchtime on the same day and the Headmaster, George Hargreaves, was sitting behind his desk in his office study, working his way through a sandwich made by his wife Ethel, consisting of Mother's Pride white bread, corned beef, cheddar cheese and tomato. The combination was not taxing on his dentures and fragments tended not to find their way underneath the plates, as was the case with sliced chicken or canned tuna. When he had finished he put away the Tupperware container in which the sandwich had been stored into his briefcase, turned his chair around, fired up his Bull Moose pipe and stared contentedly out of the window at the well-trimmed lawn in front of Southwood School.

Hargreaves was three years short of retiring on a very decent pension, after nearly forty years in the teaching profession. Now, of course, he did no actual classroom work, but oversaw the workings of the whole school, and he imagined his headmastership to be one of benevolent military authority: as he moved amongst his four hundred or so pupils like a respected Field-Marshal, inspiring awe and affection in equal measure. Occasionally he was obliged to use his cane, but only rarely and for the most grievous of infractions that were reported to him, and he wielded the tool with little enthusiasm. Use of the cane was confined to the Headmaster and the Deputy Headmaster, and Hargreaves had the sense that his own Deputy, Mr. Lupford, was too swift to resort to it. And Lupford, though in his middle-fifties, was a lifelong bachelor.

No, Hargreaves reflected, it was not the boys who caused him undue concern, but the modern brand of teacher. He could easily count the number of good, solid Tories amongst them on the fingers of one hand. Lupford, of course, was one (though it was all he had in his favour), and Hambleton (who had steadfastly refused to join any union) of the chemistry department another. But, as for the rest, they were a seething mass of socialism, communism and liberalism restlessly waiting for the call to go on strike and picket wherever they were most needed. Most of them had come into teaching via the polytechnics or the red-brick universities, and had been mentally formed in the permissive 1960s. He had good reason to believe that they viewed him, not as junior officers might view their commanding officer, but as an ideological oppressor.

Hargreaves ran a forefinger across his white moustache, puffing more deeply on the Clan tobacco smouldering in his pipe, and looked forward, with ever more affection, towards the day of his retirement when he could properly concentrate on the vegetable patch in his back garden. The turnips, in particular, were promising ... and then his deliberations were interrupted by someone knocking at the study door.

The Headmaster swung his chair around, adjusted his M.C.C. tie, ran his fingers rapidly along the comb-over straddling his pate and removed his pipe from the corner of his mouth.

"Come," he said loudly.

Mr. Spencer sauntered in, acting as if he had just

casually entered the public bar of the local pub. Without being asked, Spencer slumped into the chair opposite, pulled out a packet of cigarettes and lit one up with a cheap plastic bic.

"Please do," Hargreaves said, acidly.

"What?" said Spencer.

"Sit down and smoke."

"I have."

Spencer looked around the study. It was, he thought, like something out of one of those M.R. James stories they showed on the telly at Christmas. All mouldering books, wooden panelling, and grim oil paintings. And old Hargreaves, like a dusty spider that had just crawled out of the creepy Grandfather clock ticking away ominously in the corner.

"And what can I do for you, Mr. Spencer?" Hargreaves asked.

"It's about that new boy Salgado," he replied.

Hargreaves replaced the pipe in his mouth and took a few puffs. He was relieved. Due to the unannounced nature of his visit, Hargreaves had momentarily been concerned that the teacher had come in to inform him the N.U.T. staff were going on strike again. He rattled around in a desk drawer, pulled out a thin file and opened it.

"Ah, yes," he said. "Here we are. Alfredo Salgado. Age fourteen. Orphaned last year. Legal guardian – ah –

his aunt Maria Salgado Solares. It's his first day, isn't it? Well, what about him?"

"He's a religious fanatic. He's got the Roman church on the brain. Won't shut up about it. He was so disruptive, I had to slipper him after my class today. Why isn't he at some Catholic school?" said Spencer.

"He was actually over at St. Jerome's before coming here," Hargreaves said. "I must say that when I interviewed the boy with his aunt he struck me as really quite an intelligent little chap, something of a prodigy. I don't see what his religion has to do with it. And we don't usually have more than half a dozen of our fellows going up to university after they leave here. We need to encourage bright, enquiring young minds."

"I'm not saying he hasn't got brains, it's just that they're working entirely in one direction," Spencer replied.

Hargreaves moved his pipe from one side of his mouth to the other, considering the issue before him.

"What, he was talking about religion or theology in your history lesson?" he said.

"No, I'm not saying that. He was challenging the historical accuracy of the set texts from a dogmatic reactionary Roman Catholic perspective," Spencer said, becoming irritated. "Or at least he tried to."

Again, Hargreaves paused, while he considered the issue. The use of the word "reactionary" had settled the matter for him.

"Well," he said, "when I was in the war I served alongside quite a few Papists. All very devout God-fearing chaps and braver soldiers for it. No atheists in a fox-hole, you know. I wonder rather whether you weren't in fact excessive in using the slipper on young Salgado. It is his first day in a new school, don't you know."

"Right," Spencer grunted, stubbing out his cigarette in the ashtray and getting to his feet sharply. "I see where I stand. Good afternoon."

The history teacher exited and slammed the door behind him.

Hargreaves turned his chair back towards the window, continued to puff at his pipe and gazed at the lush green lawn outside. His thoughts returned to the cultivation of turnips.

Ж

"How did it go?" said Alan Vickery, as Dennis Spencer came into the staff-room. He scarcely needed an answer since the disgruntled expression on the history teacher's face spoke for him.

"Useless," Spencer replied. "He started talking about the bloody Second World War again. He's like a stuck record."

"What did you want done with this Salgado kid anyway?" Vickery asked.

"Nothing. Well, at the very least I wanted to know what he's doing here. This isn't the right place for him. He's a nutcase and a nuisance."

"What is the right place, at his age, if not school?"

"Some bloody Spanish monastery in the Middle Ages!"

Vickery chuckled and picked back up the copy of the latest *Private Eye* he had been reading.

From somewhere over in the corner of the staffroom another voice piped up.

"Can't say I found this new boy to be a nuisance. He scarcely said a word in my class, but when he did speak it was with quite refreshing intelligence."

It was Mr. Hambleton. He smiled benignly, took off his tortoise-shell glasses and began polishing the lenses with his handkerchief. A moustachioed man in his early fifties, he was, without his spectacles on, a dead ringer for the actor Terry-Thomas.

Spencer stared blankly in his direction. Hambleton had officially been sent to Coventry. It was bad enough that he had long steadfastly refused to join the union, but things had escalated of late. No one had spoken to him since he had crossed the picket line that time the school's N.U.T. members had come out on unofficial strike when Hargreaves, the Headmaster, questioned whether free school meals for all teachers was really necessary. Hambleton had even been seen chatting to the Nazi bullyboys who hung around outside the school gates, trying vainly to sell copies of their rag. It was true that some of the thugs were former pupils of the school but that was no excuse for it. He also read, quite openly, *The Daily Telegraph*, and had even, on a few occasions, had letters printed in it defending Polaris missiles as a war deterrent.

Despite him breaking solidarity in not maintaining Hambleton's complete ostracisation, Spencer couldn't help remarking, almost under his breath:

"I doubt there's much scope for religious ideology in chemistry lessons is there?"

Hambleton didn't acknowledge the remark and went back to his crossword puzzle.

Perhaps the most annoying aspect of the man, thought Spencer, was that he didn't appear to have realised he had even been sent to Coventry.

And he had been there for six months now.

In fact, he even seemed to prefer it.

Ж

The school day was over and the boys scrambled to get out of the building and its grounds as quickly as possible, many of them piling onto buses and making the conductors, drivers and passengers journey a misery. There was not one of them who didn't regard the vast brick edifice, all in faux-Gothic at the front, like a Gilbert Scott delirium, as some kind of daily concentration camp. Only the sixth-formers and the teachers were permitted to use the main gate at the front of the building that led directly to the junction between Archway Road and Muswell Hill Road. The vast majority of pupils had to filter out via a side gate exiting onto Wood Lane. There was no telling what heights of destruction the boys might wreak upon the front lawn were they not expressly kept away from it, and it was this serene front, of the immaculate lawn coupled with the imposing Victorian façade, a unity of order and tranquillity, that the school presented to those in the outside world.

Meanwhile, at the side gate, the torrent of screaming, laughing and shouting schoolboys poured forth. Waiting there, having arrived some ten minutes beforehand, were a group of National Front activists. There were three of them, a male youth and a female youth, both in their late teens, with the other male being in his early twenties. They were selling copies of the N.F. youth publication, *Bulldog*, which was a cross between *The Beano* and *Mein Kampf.* They ignored any black or Asian students, but would try and engage the white ones in a conversation, mostly without success.

Alfredo Salgado was making his way towards the side gate when he saw the N.F. trio. Salgado was quite alone. After that business with the history teacher, Mr. Spencer, in the first lesson of the day, the rest of his classmates didn't quite know what to make of him. They were glad of the distraction provided from what would otherwise have been yet another dull class, but it was obvious to them all that Salgado was something of a freak. He was, however, not someone to be casually trifled with, and they kept their distance after he flattened Scrubs from class 3D with a blow to the side of the head when Scrubs had tried to take his rosary off him.

Rather than walking past the N.F. trio, Salgado went straight up to them and asked to see a copy of *Bulldog*.

While he was leafing through it, the oldest one of the trio, shaven-headed and dressed in a green army camouflage jacket, asked:

"Any red scum about?"

"What do you mean?" replied Salgado.

"Red scum, you know, any commie teachers in there peddling Marxist subversion?"

Salgado did not reply.

"We've got the names of most of them already," said the shaven-headed activist. "And they're going to be denounced in the next issue. Vickery, Browne,

21

Fletcher, Patel, Spencer …"

The list went on.

Salgado tried to hand back the copy of *Bulldog*.

"Keep it," said the girl. She had short, cropped hair dyed jet-black, and eye-liner like a Queen of ancient Egypt. On the left breast of her Parka coat was pinned a Wehrmacht swastika badge. "If you can't afford to pay for it, you can have it for nothing."

"I don't want it," Salgado said.

"What's the matter, are you a Jew or something?" said the last of the trio to speak, taking a step forward. He was a grossly overweight skinhead. In fact, he was such a stereotype it was farcical.

"Read it later," said the girl. "You might learn something."

"I am not interested in inciting racial hatred. It seems to me a covert ideological position as worthy of contempt as incitement to class warfare," Salgado said.

"The kid sounds like he's swallowed a dictionary!" said the fat skinhead.

The oldest of the three, Ernest Quinn, was intrigued.

"What's that wrapped around your wrist?" he asked.

Salgado unwrapped his rosary and held it in the grip of his hand.

"He's a bead-rattler, a Pope lover, practically a

22

member of the I.R.A. for fuck's sake!" said the fat skinhead.

"You Irish Catholic?" asked Quinn. There were quite a few of them about, especially in the pubs along the Holloway Road.

"No, half-Spanish," Salgado replied.

"Dago! Why don't you go back to your own country? This one's full up, geddit? No more room," said the fat skinhead.

"Shut up," Quinn said to his N.F. comrade. "Go on your way, son. Perhaps we'll run into one another again."

Quinn watched the boy as he drifted off, entirely isolated from all his fellow schoolboys. In amongst the racial nationalist texts he'd been consuming of late, courtesy of recommendations from the N.F. leadership, he'd also stumbled across a book of essays by some dead English Catholic writer called Sinclair Egremont Xavier and, although the man was something of a clown, it had to be said, parts of Xavier's political and social vision had impressed him. Not, thought Quinn, that he would ever contemplate turning Catholic himself. Never in a million years.

"Let's go down the pub," said the fat skinhead.

"Yeh, c'mon Ernie, let's all get smashed. Buy me enough snakebites and your luck could be in tonight," said the girl.

"Fuck it," said Quinn. "Why not? Then later on back to my gaff. I've got a copy of that bootleg L.P. of White Boss, and the Dentists, at the Rock Against Communism gig. And a fridge full of cans of Double Diamond."

"Nice one. Let's finish up here first."

The three of them shouted in unison.

"Keep Britain White!"

And then, repeated half a dozen times:

"The National Front is a white man's front! Support the National Front!"

With that last shout of defiance aimed over the school gates, the three of them sloped off.

They had given away six copies of *Bulldog* but not actually sold any. The struggle would go on.

CHAPTER TWO

MARIA Salgado Solares was pleased with the continued development of her nephew under her tutelage. That he was a child prodigy, of the order of a Mozart, was beyond any doubt. When she had arrived in England, just under a year ago, she knew Alfredo only by what information rare letters from her late sister had contained. And these were usually casual references to his insatiable bookishness. Aunt Maria it was, under the grace of God, who had taken that bookishness and channelled it into the right direction, and she it was who had brought him back to the true Faith. She had begun by taking him to Mass every Sunday and on the Holy days of Obligation, seeking, wherever possible, the old Latin Rite. Then she had discovered the existence of Father Laker's Pope St. Zosimus Chapel tucked away on

Orchard Road very close by. It had been on the verge of closure, but her timely donations had kept the church going. And Alfredo had been confirmed there two months ago, an event that accelerated his devotion to Our Lord, Our Lady and the Saints in Heaven. Now he went weekly to confession, searching his conscience scrupulously beforehand, and prayed the rosary each day without fail. He could even list all the Popes, in their correct order up until Pius XII, beyond which point he admirably refused to continue.

Maria's faith had been tested much in the past. Both of her parents had died within months of one another in 1975, the same year as the death of the Caudillo, and after which Catholic Spain rapidly went to hell and all the former disgraces returned. The signs of the times had been there ever since the abomination produced by the Second Vatican Council.

The death of her husband, Armando Solares, of a sudden heart attack in 1977, had left her a widow in her early forties without children of her own. She had resolved to become a bride of Our Lord, abandon the secular world and live a life devoted to prayer, and entered the nunnery outside Valencia for instruction. She was about to complete her novitiate when she learned, in 1980, that her brother and, so too, his feckless wife, had died in a car crash, leaving her Alfredo's sole surviving relative. In her time in the convent, she discovered that the nuns of the order had been infected by Vatican II, and were more interested in obtaining the wealth she brought with her to finance renovation of the outbuildings, so she prayed for wisdom, reaching the conclusion that she would become not only the boy's legal guardian but also his guardian angel, and thus did not take her final vows. She left for London with just the contents of a suitcase and a huge bank balance from the generous inheritance left by her parents and from her husband's life insurance.

Her brother, Miguel Salgado, had strayed far from the Faith, and had met his English wife, Alfredo's mother Denise Forbes, in 1966 while she was holidaying on the Costa del Sol. The holiday romance turned into a scandal in the Salgado family when Miguel, a few weeks after she left, pursued her to London and, in doing so, did not undergo his required period of national service in the army. And he remained in England thereafter.

The whole business was ironical in one respect. For almost the reverse thing had happened to Miguel and Maria's parents thirty years earlier. Carlos Salgado, their father, had been a journalist covering British affairs and based in London until the Spanish Civil War broke out, when he returned to his homeland to fight for the Nationalists against the Republicans, but with an

English wife in tow he had acquired after a similar whirlwind romance (despite fierce resistance from his bride's parents who disavowed her as soon as the short engagement was announced).

Thus both Miguel and Maria had been brought up in an Anglo-Spanish household, albeit one devoutly Catholic, for their English mother, Florence Smith, had embraced the Faith with the fervour often displayed by converts and proved to be even more orthodoxly pious than her husband. Both English and Spanish were spoken in the home and Maria grew up knowing only of the England that existed before the Second World War, and what she saw of it in the few old black and white British films that played at the local cinema, or, much later, on the Spanish television channel T.V.E. Her English mother had harboured no desire to return to her native land, even on holiday, saying that the curtain had fallen for good on that part of her life and she was now a loyal Spaniard.

Having known next to nothing of England through direct experience before coming over to settle there, she expected, upon arrival, to find a country much like the depictions in the films and books. She imagined a land of church spires and cities of ancient architecture wreathed in fog, populated by highly conservative gentleman and prim ladies of impeccable manners who were always sitting down to take tea and crumpets.

When she actually discovered, less than an hour after arrival at London Heathrow Airport, that England had degenerated the same way Spain had done after Franco's death, but was some ten years or so even further along the same grim path, she felt betrayed. True, the current Prime Minister, Margaret Thatcher, was making a valiant attempt to stop England falling to the Bolsheviks, but without God and Holy Mother Church as her guide. Indeed, the so-called priests of England seemed very much to be the heirs of the notorious Johnson, Red Dean of Canterbury, who had openly agitated in Spain for the Republicans, and like him, more steeped in Leftism and Atheism than Traditionalism and Sacramentalism. And, Maria discovered, to her alarm, this was not only a Protestant phenomenon. Many English Roman priests were openly infected by Modernism or even outright Marxism.

This last fact was starkly brought to her attention when she had been forced to withdraw Alfredo from the local parish Catholic school. She had taken up residence in the old house she had bought in Highgate, and Alfredo came to live with her a few weeks after her arrival. She enrolled him in the College of St. Jerome after a brief, but satisfactory, interview with the elderly priest in charge of the institution, Father Maycraft, who spent most of the time reminiscing about the translation into English he had made of the poems of St. John of the

Cross forty years earlier. Moreover, he had framed photographs of Pope Pius IX, Padre Pio and Cardinal Manning adorning the walls of his study. Alas, the poor man died four months later of exhaustion. And then the trouble started.

A new priest, one Father Morgan, was appointed head of the institution. And immediately Maria was receiving reports from Alfredo of the man's heretical outrages and flagrant departures from orthodoxy and tradition. By now Maria's nephew was becoming thoroughly conversant in the heritage of his Faith, and she had stuffed his mind full with English Catholic apologists; and, towering above them all, was the Master, Sinclair Egremont Xavier. This was the author whose works Maria's mother, Florence Smith, had read to her when she was the same age. And the power of their remorselessly logical Thomism, under Grace, never wavered.

It surprised Maria not in the slightest when, a couple of weeks after he had taken over at the school, a letter arrived from Father Morgan concerning Alfredo and requesting an urgent interview with her. The typewritten text ran as follows:

Fr. Jim Morgan, S.J.
St. Jerome's College
Highgate Hill N.6.

Dear Mrs. Salgado Solares,

Please urgently arrange to visit me here at the school after 3.40 on either Thursday or Friday of this week. It is important that we have an open and frank discussion together about the recent conduct of your nephew. Please telephone the school secretary on 470 3899 to confirm our appointment.

Yours etc.,
Fr. Jim Morgan

But the interview had proved to be a fiasco. Maria entered the office and summed up the situation in a matter of moments. Father Morgan appeared to be drunk. The man was in his early forties, plump, and goggled at her lewdly from behind round granny glasses. He was not dressed appropriately—as befitted his sacerdotal position—but in a shapeless pair of beige Farah slacks and in a garish Pringle cardigan accompanied with a striped tie that was markedly askew.

"Hello Mrs. Solares, thank you for coming to see me," he said, trying surreptitiously to conceal what Maria strongly suspected was a bottle of spirits in the bottom drawer of his desk. She let the "Solares" error pass. Few English knew that a Spaniard, even a married woman, is commonly addressed by the first of her two surnames.

"Good afternoon Father," she replied.

"Call me Jim," he said. "Please do sit down."

"Thank you *Father*," she said with emphasis.

Father Morgan wished he hadn't decided to sink three quick gins before meeting this woman. It had gone straight to his head, since he'd scarcely had anything for lunch. He hated scenes and this interview was likely to be awkward, hence his resort to an old technique to calm the nerves. Now that she was standing there in front of him Morgan could see quite clearly why Alfredo Salgado behaved as he did. The priest was reminded, looking at her, of some Medieval Iberian Infanta. She was dressed all in mourning black, with a lace mantilla over raven-coloured hair. Morgan calculated her age as being somewhere in the early forties. A few crow's-foot lines marked the corners of her dark eyes, but otherwise her face was without wrinkles, and her skin was remarkably pale and translucent for someone who hailed from the Mediterranean and had been subject for many years to the rigours of its fiercer sunlight. She may even have been regarded as attractive were it not for a certain hauteur in her natural expression, a feature which tended to put one immediately ill-at-ease. It was as if she had stepped out of a portrait painting from the Spanish Golden Age of Art.

Maria, meanwhile, whilst being surveyed, was surveying herself the changes to the study that Father Morgan had made since taking over from the elderly Father Maycraft. The old flock wall-paper had been stripped away, the walls beneath painted a harsh brilliant white, and the tasteful former furniture taken out to be replaced by flat-pack replacements and cheap fabrics. Only the old filing cabinets remained. Her eyes narrowed when she saw that the former framed photographs had been replaced with new ones; all the Popes and saints were banished, and now Maria gazed incredulously at a succession of images of Father Morgan associating with what appeared to be the likes of television celebrities or pop stars at charity events. She did not recognise any of them. However, her acquaintance with modern popular music extended only so far as the likes of such lewd Spanish vocalists as Julio Iglesias and Joan Manuel Serrat. As for the television, although she owned a small black and white portable set, it was turned on very rarely, since it was clear that the Devil had got hold of the minds of those controlling the B.B.C. and I.T.V. Once, in a spasm of boredom, she had switched the device on one evening and watched a few minutes of some debased programme called "The Benny Hill Show". Thereafter, she covered the set with thick black cloth, of the type one drapes over a parrot cage in the evening.

She could not help being reminded of the egregious Mr. Hill of the television world when she looked at Father Morgan, who was still goggling at her offensively from behind his granny glasses.

"Well, I've asked you here to talk about Alfredo," he said.

"Is there a problem with his schooling?"

"Look, I'll come right to the point. I think the boy is disturbed. He seems to regard himself as some sort of smart alec who can't be taught anything and whose purpose in being here is to correct others, even me, in the error of their ways."

Looking at Father Morgan, Maria was not surprised.

"Actually," she replied, "he is a genius."

"I'm not denying that he's clever. His brains are impressive. But it's all … well, with him, it's all a kind of remorseless logic coupled with a photographic memory, without any allowances for human nuance behind it."

"And so?" she said.

"He doesn't interact with the other pupils, doesn't make friends. In fact he appears to despise them, and they're his fellow children of God. This isn't the Christian way. I've tried to talk with him about it, but he doesn't regard it as sinful at all. He sees his actions in terms of scourging, like Jesus did with the money lenders in the temple."

Still the priest was goggling at Maria and she had the distinct impression he was looking at her bust.

"So," Maria said. "He emulates the example of Our Lord! And he possesses the beautiful logical mind just like St. Thomas of Aquinas! How does that make him, as you say, disturbed? No, Father, that is not right. It is not right at all. My boy Alfredo is too good for this college!"

"What do you mean?"

"He should already be in a junior seminary for priests, it is obvious," she said. "He is very likely to make an excellent Cardinal, at least."

"I see no signs, at this stage, he has any pastoral vocation, though perhaps the Trappists might be able to do something with him, ha ha … Ahem. Still, I realise it is very early in his development and …"

"And nothing," Maria interrupted, finally standing up. "I am withdrawing him from this den of Modernism! We shall not apostatise, *Father* Morgan, no never, despite your incitements, but Alfredo's boyhood religious instruction will be my concern hereafter. His secular education can be left to the state. And when the day dawns, and it will, that the name of Alfredo Salgado is known to the honour of Catholics everywhere, yours will be forgotten!"

"This has got rather out of hand," Father Morgan replied, but before the sentence was finished Maria Salgado Solares had swept imperiously out of the room.

He reached down to the bottom drawer of his desk, pulled out the bottle of gin and poured himself a large measure. Perhaps it was for the best. He had no stomach for a repeat performance of that type, and it would be bound to re-occur in the future if Alfredo remained at St. Jerome's. What a remarkably odd woman. She was worse than the boy. The priest hoped she hadn't noticed him staring once or twice, inadvertently, at her bust.

Ж

And so Maria Salgado Solares searched around for another school for Alfredo in the state sector. She considered the idea of one of the grand old public schools, such as Eton or Harrow, but since the boy was now fourteen, it was too late for that, and the additional expense would be a waste. In any case, he was destined to become a priest and thus it was not this stage of his education that was paramount, whichever secondary school he attended.

Southwood School was located only half a mile from the Salgado household in Highgate and was convenient for that reason alone. Moreover, when Maria went to see the Headmaster, Mr. Hargreaves, she found him to be a very agreeable English gentleman. He stood up sharply when she entered his study, rushed across the room to offer her a seat and generally acted with the greatest kindness and proper courtesy. His study, Maria noticed, had retained all the decorative charm of antiquity, with panelled walls, an ornate Grandfather clock, and splendid peaked Gothic windows, the glass latticed, and providing a delightful view onto the expanse of the immaculate front lawn. So unlike the study of Father Jim Morgan.

"My dear lady," Hargreaves said, when the brief interview was concluded, "I am certain your nephew Alfredo will fit in perfectly well here. His eleven plus grades were all excellent and we will put him straight into the highest class stream of his year."

"Will you need to see him in person before he's accepted?" Maria replied.

"Not at all, not at all. We'll have him start at the school first thing next week. I'll get the school secretary to arrange the details and you will have a letter of confirmation in a couple of days."

Hargreaves' thoughts were drifting towards the vegetable patch in his back garden and the possibility of growing King Edward potatoes. His wife Ethel had insisted the water tap to the sprinkler system needed to be mended properly, though he couldn't see what the problem was. She was always calling in the same plumber to do odd jobs. Ethel said he looked just like the actor Robin Asquith. Whoever he was.

"I must have it understood that Alfredo's religious instruction is to be solely my concern. We are very strict Catholics."

"Quite so," said Hargreaves who was filling his pipe. "Aside from the little Christian homilies I dish out at weekly assembly, there is only one weekly class of religious instruction on the curriculum. Nothing formal. It is strictly non-denominational. But he can be excused from it, if you so wish."

Maria was staring at him with narrowed eyes.

"Forgive the pipe. It is a filthy habit but my sole vice," Hargreaves said, smiling.

There was an uncomfortable pause.

The eyes narrowed further.

He tamped the tobacco down with a calloused right thumb and slipped the now-extinguished pipe back into his jacket pocket.

The eyes re-assumed a normal aspect.

"Well, that seems to answer all my questions Mr. Hargreaves. I am grateful. I shan't detain you from your busy schedule. Thank you so much."

"So, we'll see the boy next week?"

"Yes indeed. Thank you again."

She got up to leave and Hargreaves raced across the study to open the door for her. He made something of an awkward bow as he showed her out.

After she'd departed he re-lit his pipe and puffed away contentedly. Perhaps Maris Pipers might be better than King Edwards though. The sprinkler thing was complex. It was, to paraphrase his favourite fictional detective, not just a three-pipe problem but more than that; a poor-pipe problem. He would have to mention this witticism later to Ethel over supper. She would, he was sure, very much enjoy hearing of it after spending a long hard afternoon with that muscular plumber.

Ж

Just over a week later Maria was waiting indoors at her house on Causton Road for Alfredo to return home after his first day at Southwood School.

She was having tea and cake with Father Nathaniel Laker, the notorious crypto-Sedevacantist priest. Laker had been exclusively offering the Tridentine Mass for a few years now at the Highgate chapel, which acquisition his loyal parishioners had privately funded at the height of the publicity caused by Laker's defiance of the church hierarchy's insistence that the *Novus Ordo* Mass of Vatican II be made available in his parish.

Since that huge wave of enthusiasm in the mid-1970s, when the chapel on Orchard Road was full to standing room only (on both Sunday Masses) and when the Faithful even had to stand outside, hearing the old rite through loudspeakers, the congregation had rather faded away. They had drifted back to the huge Victorian pile on Highgate Hill, leaving only a rump of around a dozen at Laker's chapel and a crisis as to its continued existence. Some ascribed this falling off in numbers not to a lack of enthusiasm for the Latin Mass, but to Father Laker's fiery sermons in which, for example, he claimed the Papacy had been in the hands of the Freemasons since at least 1958.

These ideas, to Maria, were not at all extraordinary. She had often read in the Spanish papers during the 1960s that Franco, the *Caudillo*, had himself expressed similar concerns about the likelihood of there having been some kind of a Masonic takeover in Holy Mother Church. Her own personal experiences led her to much the same conclusion. But she would not apostatise.

So when she had discovered the chapel on Orchard Road, spoken with Father Laker, and discovered he was loyal not only to the Tridentine Mass but also to all the infallible doctrines, she felt, at last, some force of traditional righteousness still fought back against the corruption endemic to modernity. Moreover, Alfredo had been delighted with the chapel too. She could not help feeling that the guidance of Father Laker would provide him with the correct male role model to assist in his upbringing.

"And you think Southwood School quite suitable for Alfredo?" said Father Laker as he made short work of yet another slice of fruitcake.

"He has to get a general education and exam qualifications somewhere Father," Maria replied, "and at least the school isn't a – what is the English phrase? – a wolf in sheep's clothing, like the College of St. Jerome. His religious instruction will continue as before. Orthodox and traditional."

Father Laker nodded in a sagely fashion. What little he had gleaned about state schools was that they turned out a succession of poor warped creatures that were better suited in life to be militant trade union representatives or violent inmates of mental wards than useful Catholic servants of God. Still, he would not gainsay her. He appreciated the refreshing enthusiasm both Alfredo and Maria had injected into his dwindling flock. She had already given very generously to the chapel fund and was vigorous in her piety. He did wonder, however, what with her being a Spaniard, whether she had some sort of hidden Opus Dei connection in her past. He hadn't questioned her on the subject yet, but it nagged away in the back of his mind.

"You've certainly added quite a bit to the – umm – interior adornments in your sitting room since last I visited you," he said, looking around him at the ornate crucifixes, books on Catholicism, plaster statues and portraits of Saints, and a vast range of huge Cathedral candles. The number of such things seemed to have at least doubled, as if they were reproducing by binary fission. The room looked like the inside of one of those gift shops you found outside a catacomb church in Jerusalem.

"Most was recently shipped over from the house of my parents in Valencia, after the sale of the property had been completed," she said sipping at her tea.

"You weren't tempted to stay in Spain, and bring Alfredo up there?"

"The country is now in the hands of the Reds, Father. It is ten times worse over there than here in England, where God knows, it is still bad enough. The Old Spain is finished. All the rats in the cellars that the *Caudillo* kept down are now running riot – the Basque terrorists, the communist party, the Catalan separatists – and the last hope disappeared earlier this year when Colonel Tejero's brave last ditch stand for a return to tradition was thwarted."

"Ah yes, I recall reading about that in the newspapers and seeing the biased reports on the B.B.C. television news. A great shame, a great shame. All of European civilisation is being disintegrated from within. Where once the Church stood fast against the rot, now it acquiesces in the process of corruption. In its

43

greatest epochs the Church would have declared its full support in one voice for such a man as Colonel Tejero. But, alas, no longer. These are times of tribulation."

There was something of a longish pause.

"They say that John Paul II will make the first Papal visit to this country next year," Maria said.

Father Laker blanched a little and the fragment of fruitcake in his gullet momentarily resisted final descent into his stomach. Officially, he was still in full communion with Rome. However, his view on the current Pope, indeed, on all the Popes since Pius XII, was a delicate matter.

He had not come out directly with his claim that the Chair of Peter could conceivably be vacant since the start of Vatican II, but he implied it as much as he could without provoking his own laicisation. He did not want to end up in the outer fringes of the innumerable schismatic sects who took the name "Catholic" somewhere in their nomenclatures, and who inevitably degenerated into a series of autocephalous dead ends and *episcopi vagantes.*

"That scarcely surprises me," Father Laker finally replied. "Another publicity stunt in the age of television. We can only pray that the Holy Father be guided by the Holy Ghost rather than the Modernists. There have been great storms that have assailed the Church in the past, and this is another to be weathered. One can't just take to the lifeboats like Lefebvre and his S.S.P.X."

In fact Father Laker could not forgive the present Pope for having fostered the current Indult situation in which mere tolerance of the Tridentine Mass with the ubiquitous *Novus Ordo* Mass formed a kind of half-way house. The central mystery of the Catholic Church – its Holy Mass – was turning into little more than a weekly pantomime performance accompanied by guitars, the wailing of ghastly singers, and the offering of the blessed sacrament directly into the dirty hands of non-kneeling pseudo-agnostics, half of whom never bothered with confession and even regularly used contraceptives. Only a full reaction to the reforms of Vatican II could turn back the devil's tide, and not a compromise. He longed for a Vatican III in which all the Modernism that had crept in since Pius X would be dogmatically decreed as anathema forever, world without end.

Maria watched Father Laker as he sipped at his tea. He was lost in his own thoughts again. She couldn't help noticing how often he would slip into a reverie and one of the signs he was about to do so was when he began to breathe more deeply. The process was quite disconcerting. During the middle of his meditations he tended to sound like one of those obscene phone callers she learned were plaguing women across England. He was invariably oblivious to this strange quirk he possessed. It was so bad as to prompt concern as to whether he might not get into serious trouble, by mistake, if he were to undergo an acute form of it while using the telephone.

It really was a defect he should seek to address. In other particulars he was the model of a true priest. He dressed soberly and correctly, wearing his black cassock at all times, with immaculately polished black brogues peeping out from the hem, like a spiritual soldier of Our Lord, never off-duty for a moment. It was difficult to determine his age, which may have been anything from forty to fifty, and the salt and pepper colouring of his closely cropped hair did not answer the question. His lean and angular frame told of regular fasting, while the worry lines on his forehead told of deep powers of concentration that were doubtless devoted to intense prayer.

Actually, Father Laker, thought, now almost oblivious to his surroundings, there should be a scourging. Hans Kung, Pierre De Teilhard, Karl Rahner – the whole pack of Modernist heretics – should be denounced as apostates at each Mass in every Catholic Church across the world. What he would have done to the bodies of those who supported the cause of Liberation Theology, that gang of Marxist priests who fermented revolution across Latin America, was a thing he could not bring himself to visualise in full, but it would be all the better for the salvation of their souls.

Maria had had enough. Father Laker was now snorting like a horse in a paddock. A vein in the side of his temple was pulsing ominously.

"Father!" she said loudly, attempting to bring him out of his trance-like state. "Father!"

No sooner had those final words been uttered than the door flew open and Alfredo hurtled inside.

The youth had arrived home a few minutes ago, quite silently, letting himself in with his latchkey. Upon hearing noises in the sitting room he had delayed announcing his arrival, listening outside the door in order to ascertain the identity of the guest his aunt was entertaining.

Ж

After regaining his composure and passing a few words of pastoral encouragement to the boy, Father Laker left hurriedly, citing a pressing engagement with another of his needy flock. Alfredo could not help but notice the priest had consumed all but a few crumbs of the fruitcake and that there was no more of it forthcoming.

Maria gave him some bread and jam, as well as a glass of orange squash to tide him over until supper. While he consumed the refreshments she started in on the topic that had been the main focus of her thoughts.

"Well, Alfredo, *sobrino*, how was your first day at your new school?"

"Terrible," he replied. "Most of the teachers seem to be in the pay of Moscow."

Maria expected this response. She knew that there were going to be inevitable drawbacks to her decision to send him to a state school.

He chewed, somewhat desultorily, at the crusts of the bread. His pug-like jaw worked up and down. And then he lost interest in the food.

"I was forced to correct the egregious anti-Spanish Whiggism of one so-called history teacher who then proceeded to beat me with a plimsoll after the class," he continued.

The experience did not, Maria noticed, appear to have caused Alfredo any emotional distress. He referred to it as someone might do to a minor inconvenience, like a stubbed toe. She had learnt from the beginning that it was impossible to get any idea of her nephew's emotional concerns, since they appeared not to exist. He seemed to deal only in a universe of pure ideas, of actual events and of logical causes and effects. Father Laker had suggested to her once that this was a consequence of the loss of both parents, and that in time Alfredo would heal emotionally, but there had been no change in him during the year she had spent caring for him. He regarded demonstrations of both anger and love with equal indifference, as if they were philosophical shortcomings.

Alfredo was staring at her. She had the disconcerting impression that he could divine her thoughts. And then apropos of nothing, that is, of nothing she had actually said, he stated:

"We must remember the wisdom of Socrates, whose persecution at the hands of the democratic mob so curiously prefigured the persecution of Our Lord and Saviour."

"What about the rest of the day?" she said. "Did you make any friends?"

"I fear not. The pupils are even worse than the teachers. They are little savages. But you need not concern yourself about my being the subject of bullying or anything of that nature. An early demonstration of brute force – judiciously applied – in their ranks curtailed any such tendency."

"I see," she said. "Well, that's good. And that's all?"

"There was an intriguing coda to the school day when I encountered a group of British national socialists outside the gates. They were trying, rather incompetently, to foment race war with a cross between a tabloid newspaper and a comic book."

"Hmm," Maria said. Disappointment was etched in her face. She began to wonder if she had not thought too highly of Mr. Hargreaves at their interview and too lightly of the consequences of Alfredo attending a secularist state school.

"I was, however, quite taken with the front lawn. It seems to me to be very much to Southwood School's merit. Quite immaculate."

He took a long final gulp of his orange squash, and pushed his thick, black-rimmed glasses back up along the bridge of his stubby nose. Then he unknotted his school tie.

"May I be excused?" he said. "I wish to read a chapter or two of Xavier's *Holy See or Modern Babel* in my room. I also have to say the rosary for the conversion of Mr. Spencer, our heathen history teacher."

"Yes, dear Alfredo," she replied. "You are excused. And change out of your school uniform. I will look in on you in a hour or so."

She solemnly began to clear away the cutlery and crockery from the sitting room table. Well, she thought, the first day at a new school is usually the worst.

CHAPTER THREE

DENNIS Spencer was sitting alone in the Woodman pub a few weeks later. The rest of the staff, and even (much to Spencer's surprise and chagrin) Alan Vickery, had gone instead to the Dorchester Tavern further down the road for drinks after the end of the school week. It was Hambleton's birthday and he had arranged for all the drinks (up to twenty quid) to go on his tab behind the bar. Amazingly, this bribe had dissipated in one stroke the former ostracisation that had been in effect against him for months, which, in any case, he had been too self-absorbed to apparently notice.

Spencer was not so easily conned. He recognised the game Hambleton was playing and saw it as one more move in the political chess match between progress and reaction. He would simply wait it out at the Woodman until Hambleton's credit at the Dorchester was exhausted and the likes of Vickery *et al* came back to the Woodman pub. Solidarity was stronger than capital. As he sipped at his pint of Double

Diamond and chain-smoked B&Hs his mind wandered elsewhere, to another nagging problem.

Over the last few weeks, he had observed Alfredo Salgado's behaviour at Southwood School settle down into a state of sullen resistance. The boy no longer spoke up in class to contradict the history teacher but merely adopted a series of disgruntled facial expressions when it was clear that he was not at all in agreement with certain facts Spencer taught. Salgado confined open defiance to the essays he was asked to produce, which invariably took the same pro-Catholic stance, and reached a peak of sectarianism when the course reached the subject of the Glorious Revolution of 1688. Salgado's essay on this matter was a ferocious onslaught against what he saw as a Dutch protestant invasion aided by robber Barons in the English parliament who had committed high treason to line their own pockets and to smash the sacramental liberty that a Catholic Kingship would have guaranteed to its subjects. He ended by declaring that the Glorious Revolution (he titled his essay "The Deadly Orange Invasion") was the final triumph of the Mammon idol, paving the way for the hell of the Industrial Revolution.

As well as "The Deadly Orange Invasion", Spencer also chuckled over the other egregious titles Salgado chose for his essays, such as; "James I: The Evil Oath" and "The Murderer of the Mass: Oliver Cromwell".

53

In one sense, Spencer had quite come to enjoy reading Salgado's diatribes. They were almost flawlessly constructed and he possessed a good, readable prose style. Moreover, he could predict in advance what line the boy would take and it amused him to see his predictions fulfilled every time. Naturally, the boy was not getting this stuff from a vacuum and, after a Saturday trip to the local library, where he consulted some encyclopedias, Spencer reached the conclusion that Salgado was regurgitating Sinclair Xavier's discredited hack books of history and Catholic propaganda.

Thereafter, armed with this insight, he added a few scribbled lines after marking them with the usual D grade he scrawled at the end of all Salgado's essays: "You have got this from Xavier" or "So says Xavier". And, in fact, Spencer had taken out of the library some of the dead author's books, and an old biography of his life, so he could pursue the plagiarisms further.

He found the man's whole outlook repugnant and offensively reactionary, and he could see easily why, even as far back as the 1930s, the likes of George Orwell had recognised that the entire boozy gang of Catholic pen-pushers were an irrelevance. With theology ruled out as meaningless jargon, only ideology remained, and the real choice was between socialism or fascism. Prime Minister Thatcher might have drained away some of the support for the National Front in the last election, but all it indicated was the continued link between the two factions. The Tory party was as riddled with Nazi sympathisers currently as it had been back in the 1930s. At any moment the likes of Enoch Powell could be pressed into service again and the stiff mask of Toryism would be ripped off to reveal the evil fascist deformity beneath.

Christ, they were taking their time down at the Dorchester. He glanced at his new digital watch. Over two hours had now passed. Not one of them had come back up the hill yet to join him. As if by magic, no sooner had this thought crossed his mind than he was tapped on the shoulder from behind by someone. Ah, he thought, good old Alan Vickery wouldn't leave a fellow comrade in the lurch drinking alone, and had finally had enough of drinking at the Dorchester with Hambleton and listening to the man drone on about the dangers of unilateral nuclear disarmament.

"Ha!" he said, as he turned around. "Couldn't keep away, eh?"

But the words died in his throat. It was not Vickery standing there but Dorian Marsh. Spencer groaned as if he had just received the last of three wishes from the Monkey's Paw.

Dorian Marsh was the local professional occultist. As far as Spencer could gather (that is, very little) most people involved in the occult were pretty keen to keep quiet about the subject. But this particular practitioner of the 'Secret Art' was more like a Jehovah's Witness going door to door handing out copies of *The Watch Tower*. He was in the local newspapers every other week, a mine of journalistic copy for antics involving things spectral and menacing occurring all over north London.

His emaciated form was wrapped in his customary grey raincoat with the collar turned up, bell-bottom trousers and white plimsolls. He had a pale, horse-like face, with oily brown hair plastered across his forehead. A large pentacle amulet dangled conspicuously over the front of his raincoat. Copies of his latest self-published pamphlets jutted from one of the outside pockets. An unlit cigarette dangled from one corner of his mouth.

Spencer was horribly defenceless. The curse of the Woodman pub was to be drinking without companions, when Marsh ascended from his cellar flat after dark, having finally slept off last night's hangover, seeking a lone drinker as his next victim. Spencer had made the fatal mistake of once buying him a drink towards the end of a boozy session with the rest of the teachers from Southwood School and Marsh had never forgotten it.

"Do what thou wilt shall be the whole of the law," Marsh said.

Spencer again groaned inwardly.

"I guess," Marsh went on, in his thick Cockney accent, "you don't mind if I join you?"

Then a smile crept across his features. It was the sort of creepy grin, Spencer thought, that a sex-maniac cook in an isolated convent might make after having laced supper with an infallible aphrodisiac.

Without waiting for a reply Marsh sat down, stopped smiling and goggled at him, placing the pint of bitter in his hand on the table.

Spencer shuddered.

He looked into his glass. There was only a trickle of lager remaining in it. He could get himself a drink without offering Marsh one though, who still had a full pint.

"Well, I see you're OK for a drink so I'll only get myself ..."

He stopped short as he looked up.

Marsh's glass was empty.

At the corner of his mouth the cigarette had vanished and a thin dribble of bitter all the way to his chin replaced it.

"Very kind of you to offer," said Marsh. "Just a double Jameson's for me."

Spencer sloped off to the counter to get the drinks, giving the occultist the chance to also start in on the teacher's cigarettes.

When Spencer returned with the drinks Marsh

laid the pamphlets he carried in his raincoat out on the table like a series of Tarot cards. They were photocopied and stapled publications, all reproduced in black and white, with what looked like Letraset Gothic headers. Each was around thirty pages. Spencer glanced at the covers.

"These publications," Marsh said, "are the gateway to other dimensions not only of matter, but of power, and the mysteries of ... um ... the mind."

Each one was priced at a quid.

"I've already read all of these," Spencer said.

"Are you sure?" Marsh said, looking dubious.

"I'm not likely to forget them. You sent copies to the school secretary and asked to give a talk to the pupils on 'occultism as a future career path' for a fee of five pounds."

"Ah yes, and the Headmaster sent them back to me later with a bloody rude note."

"Not before most of the staff had a look at them though."

Spencer did not elaborate on the last point but he recalled how one of the pamphlets had become something of a running joke in the staff room. *London Altars of Xog-Megasoth* contained reproductions of several photographs showing Marsh and an old boiler who was completely starkers posing inside cemetery crypts whose walls and floors they'd daubed with magical symbols. Three of the photos even featured a black goat, although it may have been a taxidermic model, since it looked pretty tatty and rigid.

"Hmmm," said Marsh. "Hargreaves thwarted my true will."

He gathered up the pamphlets and shoved them back into the pocket of his raincoat. After a ten-minute droning monologue about how the wife of someone called H.P. Lovecraft – presumably a *nom de plume* designed to attract the kinky element in the occult crowd – had been rogered by the 'Megatherion' Aleister Crowley, Marsh's purchase in a secondhand record shop of some deleted Black Widow L.P., and how Marsh had finally achieved the VIII degree O.T.O., the occultist suddenly stopped blathering. He was staring intently at a podgy middle-aged man with round eyeglasses and a cardigan sitting at the bar and knocking back a gin and tonic.

"Well," Spencer said, taking advantage of the pause, having had no opportunity to speak a word until then, "I have got to be off."

Even losing face and going to the Dorchester had to be better than listening to Marsh's rubbish and having him sponge drinks and cigarettes all evening.

"Hush," Marsh replied. "That man is a priest. It's Father Morgan from St. Jerome's. His hypocritical piety disgusts me. The Catholic Church is my most deadly foe.

It represents everything that's wrong with this world. His very presence makes me want to puke in his face."

Spencer wouldn't quite have put it like that, but was in agreement with the general position outlined. Still, he wanted to get away, but before he could repeat his statement about having to depart, he saw that this Father Morgan had noticed Marsh glaring at him. The priest slipped off of the bar stool a little unsteadily and made his way over to the table. Spencer noticed that he wasn't wearing a dog collar but a shirt and tie, which seemed rather unusual. He thought all priests knocked around in uniform outside church in order to advertise their supposed superior moral and spiritual status when amidst the plebs.

"Brace yourself," Marsh hissed. "This will be a psychic clash of wills of cyclopean proportions!"

He lit for himself yet another one of Spencer's dwindling supply of cigarettes and, rather obviously, adopted an insouciant mode.

"Evening gents," Father Morgan said. "Dorian Marsh isn't it? Quite the local celebrity. Haven't seen you in church for a while ... "

"I have now risen above the level of believing that ridiculous story that God was a Hebrew carpenter born of a virgin and that he came back from the dead to save mankind from evil. Every man and every woman is their own true Star-God and saviour," said Marsh.

" ... not since that unfortunate business a few weeks ago when you asked for an exorcism to be performed on a stuffed black goat. Yes well anyway, can I get you fellows a refill? I'm sorry, I don't know your friend's name," said Father Morgan.

"Dennis Spencer. Pleased to meet you. I work over at Southwood Comprehensive. You're over at St. Jerome's College aren't you?"

"For my sins," Father Morgan replied.

"I'll have a double Jamesons," said Marsh.

"And you?" said the priest looking at Spencer.

"A pint of lager please, Father."

"Please, call me Jim."

The priest went back to the bar to get the round in and Marsh leaned towards Spencer, lowering his voice in a conspiratorial manner.

"Don't be fooled by his devious ways. That Jesuit bastard. First of all he'll have you promising to help out at the church jumble sale next week and before you know it he'll have you queuing like a zombie to eat the body of Christ every Sunday."

Spencer nodded absently. He now recalled that Hargreaves had told him Alfredo Salgado had been over at St. Jerome's College before he had transferred to Southwood School. This would be a good opportunity to find out more from this Father Morgan about the mysterious young fiend. The folks at the Dorchester

Tavern could wait a while longer.

Father Morgan returned with the drinks and sat down.

Marsh was droning on again, fuelled by whisky.

"In the Bible, in Matthew Chapter Two, it shows without a doubt that Jesus was a reincarnated Magi, probably an Ipsissimus of the Ancient Egyptian cult of Osiris, which is derived, as you know, from the lost civilisation of Atlantis, sunk beneath the waves twenty thousand leagues ... ermm ... I mean twenty thousand years ago. And when the Three Kings followed the Star it was actually a U.F.O. they were following, like the ones in *Chariots of the Gods*, piloted by the same alien astronauts from the dying planet Mars who taught the Atlantean High Priests everything they knew ... um ... and then inspired the Hindu Vedas later and ... um ..."

Spencer wondered if he would ever get a word in edgeways and have the opportunity to ask Father Morgan about Salgado when suddenly Marsh stopped mid-sentence, drained his glass in one go and exited the pub in a flash of sudden movement.

Marsh was hotly pursued out of the premises by someone who had only just walked in a few seconds ago. It was a giant of a man in a sheepskin coat. As he chased Marsh the man was shouting something about his girlfriend, obscene phone calls and putting the occultist in traction.

Spencer and Morgan exchanged wry glances and then the former spoke:

"I wonder if you could help me with something Father … I mean, Jim."

"I'd be glad to, if I can."

"You had a pupil up at St. Jerome's who I'm teaching now at Southwood's."

"Oh, really?"

"A boy of fourteen, half-Spanish, Alfredo Salgado."

The priest gave an involuntary jerk and he spilt his gin and tonic down his tie.

"Clumsy of me. Yes, I recall the boy."

"He's Catholic, isn't he?"

"Yes he is. I should say that he and his aunt are much more Roman than Catholic Christianity proper."

"What do you mean?"

"Well, as I see it, they are traditionalists who are far too much concerned with the preservation of the church as some sort of exclusive club or even a medieval liturgical museum, rather than as a vital modern force relevant to the needs of the men and women of today."

His answer sounded well-rehearsed.

"Hmmm."

But Spencer didn't understand quite what Father Morgan was getting at (how could *any* church with all its mumbo jumbo be relevant in the 20th Century?) The priest's trendy attitude reminded him of the C of E clergymen that the B.B.C. were very happy to have on air as religious spokesmen. As long as they were encouraged not to talk about anything other than redistribution of wealth they might be useful propaganda weapons in the class war.

"You're not Catholic are you?" Father Morgan said.

"Hell, no. Dialectical Materialism is more my thing."

"Ever come across Liberation Theology?"

Spencer had vaguely heard of it, but not much more, so he dodged the subject.

"Can't say I have, that much. Look, just how did you tackle Salgado?" Spencer said.

"I am not sure Salgado can be tackled. His sort of dogmatism often proves invincible. He scarcely made any attempt to conceal his disdain for everyone connected with St. Jerome's, me included."

"Presumably you didn't just turf him out?"

"No. After all, the family's Catholic. No, the boy's aunt withdrew him from St. Jerome's herself. Remarkable woman. Quite mesmeric in her own way."

Morgan was going to add "and a fine figure of a woman" but thought better of it.

"Do they still attend Mass?" Spencer said.

"Not at St. Jerome's. I understand they go to Mass at Father Nathaniel Laker's chapel on Orchard Road now."

Spencer offered to get another round of drinks in. He was finding conversation with this amiable old God-botherer surprisingly interesting. He had no idea that the Catholic Church contained such divisions. He imagined that Catholics simply obeyed whatever instructions the Pope issued, like brain-washed fascists following their Fuehrer's orders.

"And who is this Father Laker?"

"I'm surprised you haven't heard of him. He was in all the papers, although the height of his notoriety was five years ago now."

"Before my time. I was up at Manchester University then, Jim."

"Yes, of course. Well, Father Laker caused a rumpus up at St. Jerome's. My predecessor Father Maycraft, who was quite a traditionalist himself, mind you, was decried by Laker for being what he called an Indult."

"What's that?"

"A priest who accepts the *Novus Ordo* – the vernacular form of the Mass since Vatican II – whilst being allowed to offer the Traditional Latin Mass as an extraordinary form."

"But what's wrong with that? I imagine it's some sort of compromise?"

"Yes, well that's it. But Father Laker is one of those Romanists who regards anything other than celebrating the Tridentine Mass as heretical and the vernacular form as not a valid rite at all. The man's practically sectarian. The Holy See hasn't yet acted against him formally, but it can only be a matter of time. Trying to avoid more bad publicity, I suppose. Anyway, Laker stormed off and took, for a while anyway, half of St. Jerome's congregation. Eventually most of them drifted back to us. There's only a handful left with him now."

"I suppose they're mostly Irish, or Irish descent, the congregation at St. Jerome's I mean. I don't think we have a single Irish boy in Southwood."

"Mostly, but certainly not all. There's a huge Irish community around Holloway Road as you are doubtless aware. But you know, Catholic priests aren't just secret I.R.A. sympathisers. Unfortunately a lot of English folk still think we priests are really spies working to destroy English liberty from within. It's an old historical prejudice that's hard to change. Dates right back to the Elizabethan Age. Edmund Campion and so on, you understand. Jesuits."

Spencer mainly encountered the Irish in pubs. It seemed that all of the landlords, at least as far as halfway up Highgate Hill and Archway Road, were Irishmen. Unlike the solidly Irish regulars down around Holloway Road and Tufnell Park, the clientèle became more mixed the closer one got to Highgate Village or to Highgate tube station. Even in somewhere like the

Dorchester Tavern, it wasn't unusual, deep into a Friday or Saturday night for choruses of Rebel songs to be sung and for the hat to be passed around for the Republican cause. Not that this raised any qualms in Spencer. He was all for the British Army being forced to get out of Ireland altogether. One man's freedom fighter was another man's terrorist. Look at Nelson Mandela or Kitty Marion.

He noticed that the priest was quite content when silence intruded into their conversation. Rather than moving their exchange along he seemed to have the trait of waiting for Spencer to develop it on his terms. And he wondered whether this wasn't a habit Morgan had acquired after endless hours of listening to confessions. It was rather disconcerting. These unconscious habits often developed as a consequence of one's vocation. A woman he had once dated for a couple of weeks told Spencer that he had an annoying tendency to impart information as if he was talking to a callow pupil in a classroom and not to a fellow adult. Their relationship broke up shortly afterwards.

"Well," Spencer eventually said, "it appears the kid Salgado isn't quite your typical Catholic, as I thought. It doesn't seem to me that his aunt and this reactionary nutcase Laker are very good influences for him."

"That may be so. But he still has his whole life ahead of him. Life experience, rather than pure logic, also changes a person."

"You know, Father – I mean, Jim – I wonder whether all that means is that we get more selfish as we get older and try to live in the past. Towards the end that's what our lives amount to, a long past behind with no future ahead."

"There's always the younger generation."

"Who make the same mistakes unless they are educated the correct way and kept on the path of progress."

The conversation had taken a depressing turn.

Just then Alan Vickery walked in, his sojourn down at the Dorchester having ended. Father Morgan noticed Spencer's distraction and decided this would be the right moment to depart. He was feeling quite sozzled.

"Well," he said, "I had better be getting back to St. Jerome's. Our tête-à-tête has been most interesting, thank you. Lovely to meet you. I do wish you would come and see me sometime for tea or a dram. Oh, and there's a jumble sale next Saturday afternoon, you know. The T.V. newslady Angela Rippon will be there to open it. Very delightful. Charming. Super legs. Lovely dancer too. If you have any old books or the like you could donate they'd be most welcome. Let me give you my number at the church."

He scribbled down the telephone number on the back of one of the beermats and slid it across to him.

Then, after shaking Spencer by the hand, he shuffled off.

Spencer got up from the table, drink in hand, and wandered over to Alan Vickery at the bar. It was now past ten, and later than he'd realised.

"Oh, hullo Dennis, there you are," Vickery said.

"What happened to Hambleton's bash?" Spencer asked.

"Bash is the operative word. He got punched right in the gob by an Irishman."

"Really? Tell me more." He could scarcely conceal his delight.

"Everything was pretty calm until a hour ago when all the Irish hardcore regulars at the Dorchester started to drift in and the Guinness and whisky chasers started flowing. They only gave our crowd some funny looks to start with, but Hambleton, who'd had a skinful by then, started in with the Irish jokes he'd got from watching that programme 'The Comedians' that's on the telly. It wouldn't have been too bad if he'd kept it down but he's got a voice like a three-minute warning siren."

"Yeh, it's impossible to ignore."

"So, Hambleton is telling these appalling jokes and all the time our Irish friends are staring at us with increasing errm ..."

"Enmity?"

"Yes, enmity. And their numbers meanwhile are

growing. One of them, a bloke only about five foot six
but with a broken nose and cauliflower ears, who looks
like a boxer, comes over to tell Hambleton to put a sock
in it. Which he does. For five minutes. Then he switches
from telling jokes to trying to get us all to sing 'God
Save the Queen'."

"Idiot."

"By that stage, most of our crowd had quietly
slipped away. I mean, it's true that he'd stopped paying
for our free drinks, but, like me, they were probably all
too much reminded that Hambleton thinks of Keith
Joseph as being too left-wing."

"So why didn't you leave?"

"Had to report back to you in full, didn't I?
Anyway, I haven't laughed that much in ages," Vickery
said with a grin.

"Go on."

"Towards the end, Hambleton is on his feet, alone,
singing the National Anthem and I'm edging my way
out of his orbit. The now well-fuelled Sons of Erin
inside the place are gearing up for a re-run of the
Brixton riot, but Irish, not Caribbean style. Luckily the
bloke who looked like a boxer defused the situation by
dancing across the carpet and subjecting Hambleton to,
as Malcolm McDowell might put it, a little of the old
ultra-violence."

"So that was that?"

"More or less. Have you ever seen *Casablanca*?"

"Years ago. What's that got to do with anything?"

"Well, it reminded me a bit of the scene in Rick's bar with Conrad Veidt and Paul Henreid. Anyway, just before it was lights out for Hambleton one of the regulars started banging away at the piano and singing 'Danny Boy' and they all joined in, drowning out 'God Save the Queen'. Very funny."

"And what happened to Hambleton?"

"Oh, he sloped off down to the A&E department at the Whittington Hospital to get cleaned up I imagine. Internal ketchup all over his face. And I decided to join you up here before last orders."

"Want another?" Spencer said. "My shout. Doubles. Let's celebrate."

CHAPTER FOUR

THE Chapel of Pope St. Zosimus was hidden away halfway along Orchard Road, in the mazy borderland of backstreets between Crouch End and Highgate. It had once been a Baptist chapel, built in 1889, but had fallen into disuse during the 1950s and abandoned until 1976 when fund-raising by Father Laker's flock had secured the funds for its renovation, consecration and re-opening as a traditionalist Catholic place of worship. At the time it attracted a great deal of publicity, especially as church attendances were dwindling, at least across the endless Protestant denominations (and even the much more architecturally impressive Jackson's Lane Methodist church on the Archway Road had closed a few months later in the same year). At first, the Zosimus Chapel enjoyed a large congregation, greater than the modest chapel itself could contain, but now, in 1981, the number of regular worshippers had dwindled to just over a dozen, leaving the pews mostly unoccupied at Mass. The building was set several feet back from the row of terraced houses on the east side of the street, and one entered via descending a small flight of stone steps leading to its porch. It had been constructed at a sunken level one floor lower than the pavement level terraced houses. The outside of the chapel itself was generally uninspiring, being the type of simply designed box-like structure preferred by Baptists, but it possessed a modest flourish of ornamentation in the form of a vaguely Classical Grecian front, consisting of a small portico and two Ionic pillars.

However, were any Baptist to wander inside now, perhaps not having noticed the sign outside indicating it was a place of Roman Catholic worship, or even out of idle curiosity, he or she would have been staggered – perhaps even appalled – by the contrast between the interior and exterior.

The essential features common to all Catholic churches were in place, such as the tabernacle with the red flame that was continuously alight (except for the period of Tenebrae), and the twelve Stations of the Cross, following the Eric Gill designs. The décor of the place was a re-conversion to Medievalism. Light was admitted through a single stained-glass window, with a peaked arch, east facing, high up above the altar, depicting the crucifixion of Our Lord. The glass was genuinely antique, and had been salvaged from a church bombed-out during the Blitz, kept by a local private collector, and then restored and placed here into the Zosimus Chapel when it reopened. The window was so narrow that the sun's rays, upon passing directly through it, were like the fixed beam of a multicoloured searchlight. This single, central source of illumination left the remaining areas of the chapel in a perpetual twilight whose shadowy depths were only broken by the banks of flickering candles honouring the saints. The multitude of plaster statues symbolising the Apostles and Our Lady crowded the chapel. A huge handwoven tapestry adorned the upper portion of the west wall, fixed above the entrance door. The thing was faded, moth-eaten and ancient, its details near-impossible to make out, but represented Our Lord's encounter with Pontius Pilate.

An ornate, beautiful confessional box, wrought in carved teakwood, stood at the corner of the west and the north walls.

Inside sat Father Laker and Alfredo Salgado, who was the last of five of the faithful that day to make their confession before the Mass. Some distance away his aunt was saying a decade on her rosary, having made her confession previously and now making prayerful reparation for her sins, along with the other three penitents.

"Bless me, Father, for I have sinned. It is a week since my last confession. I accuse myself of …"

The boy hesitated for several seconds.

"Go on my son," said Father Laker. "There is no sin so terrible it is beyond Christ's forgiveness for those that truly seek it."

The priest had difficulty discerning whether Salgado's hesitation was a matter of shame or of confusion. His prior confessions, since confirmation, had been entirely for venal sins, for matters of ignorance and not wilful spiritual wrongdoing. Boys of his age either agonised over their impure thoughts or acts, a sin to which Salgado had apparently never succumbed, or else they were prone to making up sins simply to have something to confess.

"I accuse myself of … I accuse myself of the mortal sin of pride."

"What form does this pride take?"

Laker imagined he knew the answer before it was given. Of course it must be intellectual pride. When one knew one was surrounded by those in error, living in a world gone horribly astray, there was a temptation to glory in one's own rectitude and to look down uncharitably on one's fellow men. It was a temptation to which Laker himself had often been prey.

"I take pride in the knowledge that, since my last

confession, I have been wholly without any stain of sin, Father."

The vein in Laker's temple began to pulse and his breathing grew deeper.

"You mean you take pride in being in the state of Grace?"

"It was worst after I last received the blessed Sacrament."

"But this isn't a sin, my son. Not all pride is sin. To be spiritually reconciled with Christ is a cause for joy not sorrow."

The boy didn't answer.

"Are there any other matters troubling your conscience?" Laker asked.

"No Father," the boy replied.

"Then you are not in need of absolution. But I bless you in the name of the Father and of the Son and of the Holy Ghost."

The boy was still sitting there, silently.

"You can go now," the priest said.

Eventually, the boy did. Noisily.

Ж

Several other members of the congregation came into the church in order to pray the rosary before Mass.

There was the sound of a tinkling bell from an

indistinct source and the Faithful stood as one body. After the preparatory prayers and the credo, a cloud of white incense smoke wafted over the confines of the church interior, not sharp or soft in the nostrils but akin to the aroma of spices from a far distant land that one knew intimately from the past, an aroma both exotic and yet familiar, close at hand and yet far away, in memory and in reality. The priest, now clad in his white vestments, sanctified the offerings of the Mass with the incense and cleansed his hands in holy water.

The ancient pleas for mercy were invoked in Greek to the Lord of Hosts; *"Kyrie eleison."* and *"Christe eleison."*. And then in Latin, *"Gloria in excelsis."*

The priest kissed the altar, turned to the Faithful and said:

"Dominus vobiscum."

And the reply: *"Et cum spiritu tuo."*

The collect prayers and an Epistle of St. Paul followed, and then the chanted Gradual and the chanted Gospel.

The Credo was sung, *"Credo in unum Deum ... ET INCARNATUS EST DE SPIRITU SANCTO EX MARIA VIRGINE: ET HOMO FACTUS EST ..."*

"Amen."

The Holy sacrifice was about to begin.

"Dominus vobiscum."

And again the reply: *"Et cum spiritu tuo."*

"*Oremus.*"

Then the Offertory from Holy Scripture.

The Apostolic servant of God stood before the High Altar, his back to the Faithful, undertaking the supreme masterwork of the Holy Sacrifice instituted by Our Lord and Blessed Saviour, instituted for almost two thousand years, sustained by the Holy Ghost, across all the world, at every single hour of darkness and light, in times of war and in times of peace, in times of fear and times of hope, for each man, woman and child, for the living and the dead, for all the saints and for all the sinners.

It was for this, and this alone, that the Mass existed: as an outward sign of the Mystery of Faith and the Sacrifice of Almighty God.

Ж

When the Mass was concluded the fact that Alfredo Salgado had remained kneeling in prayer, alone, whilst the congregation had all been kneeling at the altar rail taking communion, did not go unnoticed.

Father Laker was nothing less than astonished by his behaviour, and Maria Salgado was highly alarmed. The rest of the Faithful, naturally, wondered to themselves about the nature of the awful sin the teenage boy must have committed that he could not bring himself to confess and be absolved before the

Mass, and which prevented him from taking the Blessed Sacrament.

As the rest of the flock drifted away, and Alfredo Salgado lingered outside, waiting for his aunt to emerge, she took the opportunity to speak briefly with Father Laker.

"I thought," she said, "my boy has confessed his sins to you. Surely he wasn't refused absolution?"

Father Laker was bound by the inviolate oath of secrecy that safeguards the confessional and the rite of reconciliation. The situation was a little delicate. On the one hand Alfredo had no sins that required absolution and so no confession had been necessary. On the other hand the boy had believed he required both quite clearly. It would be best to err on the side of caution and speak to him alone and in private on the matter.

"I think there has just been a misunderstanding," he replied. "Let me speak to Alfredo on Tuesday afternoon, alone, once the dust has settled, and I am sure we can clear up the confusion."

Maria looked at him rather sharply. For a moment her eyes narrowed ominously and a touch of hauteur flashed in them.

Father Laker suddenly felt as if he was in the presence of some ancient Royal patron. He was conscious, all at once, that without the financial support of this Spanish widow in the black mantilla, who was still turning over the huge scarlet rosary beads in the fingers of her right hand, his chapel could not continue. Her private donations far outstripped the meagre amount collected via the offerings of the rest of the congregation, and the chapel had no financial aid from the rest of the Roman Catholic Church. Without Salgado, he would have to consider going over formally to some well-financed traditionalist group like the Society of Saint Pius X, if they would have him.

"I will tell my boy to come to confession on Tuesday then, after school," she said, turning on her heel.

Father Laker felt as if he were being tested.

Ж

Back at the modest house in Causton Street, Maria was cooking Sunday luncheon. She knew that it was part of the traditional family order of the day in this country, and the meal became a centrepiece. She had never quite mastered the art of an English roast, and somehow always managed either to burn or under-cook the parsnips, but she had memories of her own English mother making a fuss over Sunday luncheon back in Spain, although it had been nearly impossible to obtain all the right ingredients, and they ate it in the evening, not during the afternoon, when the siesta was *de rigueur.* After the meal, her father, full in belly, exuded a sense of tranquil satisfaction that lingered over the whole evening. The thing was a gamble that always paid off. Sometimes, on Sundays, they had paella; which her mother had mastered several years earlier, and which rendered her father even more satisfied than the English roast. He had, he felt, the best of both national cuisines.

Once Maria had served the meal, said grace, and they began to eat, she realised it was another culinary disaster. The gravy turned watery in the flabby brussel sprouts. The cauliflower was too hard. The potatoes were so crispy on the outside that they had to be cracked open. The beef was chewy and stringy. After a few mouthfuls she pushed her plate away and lit a cigarette. Alfredo, however, didn't seem to notice how disgusting the food was, and devoured the muck with gusto, washing it down with a tall glass of orange squash filled with ice. The lower half of his pug-like face worked relentlessly from side to side, reducing the contents of his mouth to a digestible mess. She noticed that he didn't consume the individual components of the meal with any particular preference, or in any order, but ranged across it as a whole, as if they were all interchangeable.

Maria had the absurd idea that she might just as well have prepared a warmed up tin of dog food and some boiled cabbage, covered in instant gravy, and the boy would have noticed nothing amiss.

She stubbed out her cigarette in the rather cheap tiny blue ashtray and watched Alfredo finish his food. For dessert, she gave him a bowl of Walls raspberry ripple ice cream and allowed him to have one small glass of *Rioja*, which always made him drowsy.

Thinking back to that traditional English meal her mother had inflicted upon the family in Spain, she realised now what the intent behind it had been, at least in part, aside from the continuity it provided with an overseas heritage. On the occasions when her mother had made a special effort she could twist her father around her little finger (as the colloquial English expression put it) and it was then, and only then, that she made household suggestions he would otherwise have resisted as impertinent from a wife. The truth was, and he either did not know it, or did not want to admit it, that she was the one in charge of the family. Provided the illusion was maintained, when in outside company, that he made all the decisions, in keeping with the strict patriarchal and traditional values of a Spanish *cabellero*, then he was contented.

Maria had decided to try the same thing with Alfredo. Of course the two situations were not directly comparable, and there was no question as to who enjoyed final authority in their household, but filling up her nephew with a specially prepared meal (which he, apparently, relished), might make him more amenable to the enquiries she intended to direct at him. Alfredo's conduct at Mass had been highly unorthodox and she intended to get to the bottom of it.

Alfredo asked to leave the table and flopped over to the nearest armchair, rubbing the back of his head against the lace antimacassar, behaving somewhat like a contented dog.

Maria cleared away the table, turned on the radio set, which was tuned to B.B.C. Radio 3 (the only station she could tolerate) and, as the strains of Beethoven's *Missa Solemnis in D Major* played in the background, she dealt with the washing up in a determined fashion, scrubbing every last trace of filth from the pots and pans, and the plates and cutlery. In Spain, during the 1950s, her family had employed a maid servant, but they had moved into a smaller, modern apartment in Valencia during the early 1960s, when her father retired from his political post as Agricultural Under Secretary. And so her mother and she had taken up the menial tasks themselves, although, with the more widespread availability of household labour-saving devices, under the economic miracle of that decade, they were scarcely the burden they had been only a few decades ago.

Employment of a full-time servant was, she

thought, now largely a matter of ostentation, or else of personal sloth, except in very large homes. Contrary to the impression of grandeur she was aware she projected, it was a source of pride to Maria that she could dedicate herself to managing the house in Causton Road wholly independently without resorting to a servant. The undertaking of the domestic chores provided humility and rooted her in her belief that she had been given a prime task by God to perform to the utmost of her abilities; to provide a true Catholic home for her nephew in which he would flourish in the Faith.

She dried all the kitchen implements with a dishcloth and put them away in the cupboards and drawers.

It was time to tackle Alfredo. By now he would be a little dozy, his stomach digesting the meal and the glass of wine, and he would be most amenable to her enquiries about what had happened at Mass.

She wandered back into the parlour, where the boy was half-curled up in the armchair, listening with interest to the Beethoven concert that was being broadcast live on the radio.

"*Sobrino mio,*" she began.

"I am not at all convinced that the Romanticism of Beethoven is suitable for a solemn Mass. The music should be an organic unity, a continuum of sacred tradition," Alfredo said. "Really, only plainchant will do.

Or Gregorian chant, at worst."

She glided across the room and turned the radio set off, then sat down across from him in a wicker chair, folding her hands in her lap.

"My dear nephew," she began again, fixing his gaze with that penetrating stare she herself did not know that she possessed. "Let's talk about what happened today at your confession, shall we? Did Father Laker say anything to upset you?"

Alfredo shifted in his armchair. He said nothing. Then he polished his eyeglasses with his handkerchief. When he put them back on he closed his eyes, and yawned as if he were sleepy.

"Will you answer my question?" Maria said, her stare intensifying.

"Aunt," replied Alfredo, still with his eyes closed, and with a dreamy, half-awake tone in his voice. "You understand that's impossible for me to answer, much as I might prefer to. The matter is between me and my confessor. And God, of course."

Abruptly, she stood up. She knew technically he was right, but she had at least hoped to try and discover on whose side the cause for Alfredo's not having been absolved originated.

"I am not asking you to tell me about your sins, but about …"

She paused mid-sentence.

Alfredo had quite clearly fallen asleep. His head rested on the right wing of the armchair and he was gently snoring.

For a moment she thought of shaking him awake. Had there been an iota of impudence in his manner, or if she believed that he was play-acting, she would have done so, but neither appeared to her to be the case. He had simply fallen asleep after too heavy a meal and after giving the best answer he felt he could at the time in accordance with his conscience.

Ж

When Alfredo woke up later in the afternoon, after an hour and a half of dozing, he felt refreshed and eager to get back to his studies. He was a third of the way through a very interesting commentary on St. Anselm's ontological argument, and he was not sure what conclusion as to its logical validity would be reached.

Maria tried to re-open the subject of Father Laker with him, telling him that she had arranged an appointment for Tuesday with the priest, who was sure it was all a misunderstanding, but Alfredo repeated his former answer and then deflected the issue, by adding that he would naturally be glad to see Father Laker again for any reason.

This seemed to mollify her concerns and Alfredo

spent the rest of the evening studying alone, in autodidactic delight, up in his little attic room, which was rapidly filling up with all manner of theological volumes he had requested his aunt purchase for him.

CHAPTER FIVE

BY Monday, Hambleton's face was a delight to behold. His left eye was surrounded by a nasty bruise, the lids almost closed altogether. His top lip was puffed up and his nose covered with a dressing. As Spencer glanced at the sight over his copy of *The Morning Star* he found it nearly impossible not to smirk. Hambleton had been ribbed about it all morning by the other teachers, and even old Hargreaves was displeased with him, the words "not a good example to set the boys, old chap" having been audibly murmured.

There were only the two of them in the staff room, both having a free period just after lunch without a class to teach. Not a word had been exchanged. Spencer hadn't spoken to Hambleton for months anyway, since that business with him crossing the picket line, and Hambleton had apparently abandoned all his silly attempts to pretend not to notice he had been sent to Coventry by chattering away despite the reality. Doubtless some of the right-wing impudence had been knocked out of him by his treatment at the hands of the Sons of Erin. He was leafing through a copy of *Private Eye*, that satirical rag run by old public school boys. In the background the radio was on, and tuned to the B.B.C., which was broadcasting Prime Minister's questions from the House of Commons.

Maggie Thatcher and Michael Foot were going at one another over the unions, with the former dragging out the tired old arguments about Labour being in their pay, and with the latter sensibly pointing out that they were the only real guarantor of working class rights. Of course everyone knew that the argument had been settled when Ted Heath had tried and failed to take them on, being finally forced to accept they were an integral part of the social contract. Thatcher had no chance against Foot's superior brain, and time and again he showed her up for the petty-bourgeois daughter of a shopkeeper that she truly was. Her ratings in the opinion polls were abysmal and the novelty of having a female Prime Minister had worn off very rapidly. There was little doubt that, come the next general election, she and her government would be turfed out along with the U.S. Airforce bases, Cruise missiles, Apartheid Nazis, E.E.C. Capitalist bankers and all the rest of the Imperialist baggage that came with a Conservative administration.

Michael Foot was only the beginning. The Labour Party was only the beginning. Marxism was on the rise. Capitalism was doomed – through historical inevitability and its own inherent contradictions – to fall.

Hambleton was himself getting increasingly agitated.

He squirmed in his chair, rustling his copy of *Private Eye* and snorting.

Thatcher began squealing like a matron, the Tory M.P.s were braying wildly, and the Speaker's cries of "Order! Order!" fell on deaf ears. Foot was in full flow, his impeccable logic scoring point after point, driving the toffs and the millionaires into a frenzy of upper class, privileged contempt for the truth.

"Turn it off will you, Spencer? That racket is giving me a splitting headache," said Hambleton.

Spencer looked at him coolly but didn't reply.

Instead, he reached over to the radio and turned the volume up.

Hambleton glared at him for a second, and then got to his feet and stormed off.

Under the sound of "Order! Order!" now booming from the radio, Spencer began to whistle "The Red Flag".

Ж

At the same time, less than a mile away, Ernie Quinn ran the palm of his right hand over his shaven scalp. He would have to use the clippers on it this afternoon to keep it to skinhead regulation. Twice a week at least was the discipline he imposed upon himself.

He was sitting in his bedsit alone above the newsagents on the Archway Road. His landlord, Hugh Fitzroy, was a good man, now in his early seventies, who had marched with Mosley in the nineteen-thirties, and never gave him much trouble when he fell behind with the rent. He was a solid N.F. supporter but, like everyone else, had been dismayed when the party was routed at the 1979 election and John Tyndall had been replaced as leader, going off to form a breakaway group under the name "The New National Front". Quinn got the feeling that Fitzroy wasn't entirely comfortable with the rise of the nationalist skinhead movement. Back in his day the Front had consisted mostly of respectable men in suits, and women in dresses, rather than the burgeoning youth movement that had taken to the streets more recently and fought directly against the red menace in Britain. Nevertheless, Fitzroy obviously saw something of his own youthful enthusiasm in Quinn that reminded him of the days when he had brawled against the communists with the black-shirted British

Union of Fascists.

Once every two weeks, Friday at ten a.m., and for the past six months, Quinn had trawled down to the dole office at the bottom of the hill to sign on. He regarded the place as a nightmare. It was filled with immigrants and scroungers, queuing in front of, and working behind, the counters with their reinforced glass barriers. There were always rows over lost or late Post Office giros that were supposed to have been sent out and it was common to see the UB40 claimants screaming at the civil servants behind the glass or banging their fists on the barrier in frustration. Quinn, however, had been determined to get off the system and had finally done so. He had begun writing pieces for *Bulldog*, the N.F. Youth Publication, and had been eventually offered a role as its assistant editor, which he had taken up two weeks ago. The wage wasn't much more than the dole, but it could lead to better things. Quinn had been given a sense of purpose and direction, and felt honoured to have been chosen to serve the cause of white liberation.

Over in the corner of the bedsit, atop a card table, was his Adler manual typewriter, at which he would bang away writing articles in the morning and afternoon. These he had to deliver two or three times a week to the Front's regional office over in Teddington. It was a long and boring journey across London, but he took the opportunity to read all the books on race theory and suppression of white culture that the traitors had sought either to suppress or write out of history in their union-controlled schools and universities.

The Trots on the left claimed that fascism was a tool used by capitalism and the big business companies for their own ends, but the Tories now in government showed this to be a lie, thought Quinn. They were still jailing N.F. supporters by use of the Race Relations Act and banning the party's marches, exactly as the socialist Labour Party had done before them.

The new connections he was making as a result of his occupation were not like his old friends, who were pretty ignorant, and really only interested in the lifestyle, the music and the thrill of confrontation. Most of them could have easily drifted into other movements, following fashion and peer pressure, and didn't appreciate that there was an elite vanguard who directed activities behind the scenes which their limited horizons precluded them from reaching. All the recruitment drives outside schools, football grounds and tube stations were designed to supply the movement only with the necessary masses of foot-soldiers, who would follow the command of the leaders.

Those at the top were well-educated men, often Oxbridge graduates, and some from very wealthy families. They were, naturally, positioned outside the

Establishment, but often had contacts within its ranks. Since the disaster of 1979 and the failure of the N.F. to secure power through the ballot-box, he had learnt, from his new friends, that the only possible way to secure power was to foment race war in the same way as the Trotskyites sought to foment class war. The ensuing conflict and state of emergency would open up support from the masses for revolutionary, not democratic, change, and that process would sweep the movement to power on a wave of popular support.

History showed that it had happened before in Europe, on both the revolutionary left and the revolutionary right, and, if it happened before, it could happen again.

Ж

The following morning, on Tuesday, Maria Salgado Solares' world fell apart.

Alfredo had been sent off to Southwood School fifteen minutes ago and she was busying herself tidying up the parlour when the telephone rang.

"Hello," she said. "Who is speaking please?"

"Is that Mrs. Salgado? I'm calling about your nephew Alfredo. This is Doctor Shelley, Whittington Hospital A&E department."

She went pale and clutched at the wall for support.

"Hello? Are you there?"

She fought desperately against the desire to shriek aloud.

"Yes, this is Maria Salgado. What has happened?"

"Your nephew's been hit by a car on his way to school. You'd better come over here right away."

Ж

Much later on Tuesday, Father Laker was kneeling in front of the altar in the chapel of Pope St. Zosimus, continuing his prayers for Alfredo's recovery. Maria had telephoned him before she had left for the hospital, told him what had happened, and the priest had gone straight to the accident and emergency ward to lend what assistance he could.

The youth was in a shocking state. He'd broken several bones but it was the damage to his skull that most concerned the doctors. They suspected a blood clot in his brain caused by the trauma and he was rushed into surgery not long after arrival at the hospital.

Beforehand, Laker had given Alfredo the Last Rites, whilst Maria had recited the rosary, and then the boy had been taken into the operating theatre.

Laker and Maria Salgado prayed for his deliverance.

He'd survived the long medical ordeal, but the

surgeon told them that the next few days were crucial in his survival, and he was put into the intensive care ward, still unconscious, lingering on the edge of life and death.

It seemed that the car had ploughed into him at the corner of Jackson's Lane, and the driver sped off, without stopping. Of course the police initiated enquiries and made a public appeal for witnesses the same day but, astonishingly for such a busy road, no one had had seen the event itself occur. It was almost as if the vehicle had been waiting for Alfredo, had jumped into existence, done its job of running the boy down, and then jumped out of existence again, leaving behind as proof of its presence only Alfredo's mangled wreck. The person who called 999 had been in the telephone box opposite, on Shepherd's Hill, at the time, and reported hearing the boy cry out, but saw nothing, except for the body lying sprawled and bloody on the pavement.

Laker finished reciting his prayers, crossed himself and turned away from the altar. He made his way along the aisle, pulled the entrance door shut behind him, and the latch of the Yale lock clicked loudly across the confines of the almost pitch-black chapel. Only the dim orange light of the tabernacle, indicating the perpetual presence of the Blessed Host, pierced the darkness.

Ж

Doctor Giles Shelley was still on duty when one of the nurses, Milly Jackson, paged him from the Intensive Care Ward. Once she'd reached him, she told him, over the internal phone system, that Alfredo Salgado was showing signs of regaining consciousness. He was responding to outside stimuli but hadn't yet spoken. The thing, on first consideration, seemed incredible. The chief neurologist Mr. Davis, who had operated on the boy Salgado several hours ago, estimated that he wouldn't even begin to respond to outside stimuli for weeks, if at all. The young patient looked certain to slip into a long coma, such was the haematoma in the frontal brain lobe and the extent of inflammation across both parietal and occipital lobes.

"I thought I'd let you know first, doctor," the nurse said. "Should I advise Mr. Davis?"

Shelley glanced at his watch. It was eleven-thirty p.m. His working day had turned into an exhausting and sweaty fourteen-hour shift of patients' blood and tears. By contrast Davis would, around now, be climbing into bed with that much younger trophy wife he was so proud of displaying to the other doctors at the Christmas party.

"Not right away," Shelley replied. "Let me go up and take a look at him and I'll decide whether it's worthwhile bothering Mister Davis. It may be a very minor transitory episode of consciousness. Anomalous and nothing more than that."

"What about the boy's aunt? She was insistent that we let her know immediately of any change at all," the nurse said.

"No need to do anything like that until I've examined him for myself," Shelley said. "I don't want to give her false hope, not at this early stage."

He made his way through the labyrinthine series of sterile white-washed corridors. The further away one got from the A&E department, the more eerily quiet the whole building seemed. At that time of the night only A&E was insomniac, what with the belligerent or accident-prone drunks spilling out of pubs and straight into casualty, but the rest of the hospital could have been deserted. The patients were all asleep, either through boredom or sleeping pills, and had been for hours now, whilst half-attentive night nurses read cheap romantic paperback novels, interrupted in their private fantasies only by the patients' requests for bedpans, glasses of water, or stronger painkillers.

Shelley reached the Intensive Care ward and found nurse Jackson attending to the boy Alfredo. The patient's head was swathed in bandages and both his right leg and arm were in plaster casts. A variety of tubes and wires were connected to his body, the former supplying oxygen and saline, the latter connected to monitors that bleeped repetitively in the background.

Shelley examined him.

"He's showing signs of being able to breathe without the ventilator. Let's remove it for a minute and see how he gets on," he said to Nurse Jackson.

She did so, and Alfredo, laboriously in the first few attempts but soon in a regular pattern, began to breathe on his own.

And then his eye-lids flickered open. He stared around him at the unfamiliar surroundings and was obviously taking it all in.

Then he spoke, slowly, with the intonation somewhat slurred.

"Where am I?" What's happened?"

"You're in hospital, Alfredo. I'm Doctor Shelley, you've had a nasty accident, hit and run, but you're going to be alright."

The boy nodded.

"How long have I been unconscious?"

"Just over a day. I want you to stare at and follow my index finger as I move it. Can you do that for me?"

Alfredo nodded.

Shelley did a basic visual cognition test by making Alfredo gaze at and follow the slow movements of his index finger up and down and back and forth.

It was remarkable. The first indications were that

the boy's spatial awareness and coordination were relatively unimpaired.

"How are you feeling? Any pain, discomfort, dizziness?"

"Nothing of the sort except my right arm and leg ache, both broken I suppose," Alfredo said, looking along his body at his limbs.

"You were pretty beaten up when the car hit you. Can you remember that?"

"Didn't see it. Must have come at me like the Devil, out of nowhere. I remember the Pelican crossing was clear then … "

He coughed several times, expelling red-tinged mucus from his lungs.

"My aunt …"

"That's enough for now, Alfredo," Shelley said. "Try and get some sleep. I'm going to telephone your aunt first thing in the morning and get her over here."

"Not tired," he said. "Not tired at all. Don't feel sleepy."

"Just relax then, and settle back. Don't try and talk any more. Nurse Jackson here will stay with you."

Ж

Shelley decided not to phone Davis. The consultant wouldn't have appreciated being dragged out of bed in the middle of the night, even though the recovery of the boy Alfredo verged on the miraculous. However, such was his own excitement that he didn't want to leave the hospital himself in case further developments occurred in his absence and, so too, he had a sense of direct responsibility, the feeling that someone should be on hand. There was nothing more to do than catch a few hours sleep on a trolley down in one of the A&E examination rooms; the mad rush of the post-pub crowd having tailed off after midnight. He had done so on several occasions before. Nurse Jackson, who was on duty all night, promised to fetch him should any change in Alfredo's condition take place.

It was after two hours that Nurse Jackson came to A&E and awoke him.

"What's going on?" he said. "Any change?"

"I would have woken you before but, well, you were obviously exhausted," she replied.

"What is it? Has he slipped back into coma?"

"No, something else. I wanted to make sure first."

She glanced at her watch.

"The next episode is due very shortly. I've timed them. You really need to see it for yourself. It's easier than me explaining it. Come on."

He accompanied her to Intensive Care and the two of them stood around Alfredo's bed. The boy was fully conscious and staring at them both. He didn't appear to recognise Shelley, only the nurse.

"What is …" Shelley said and then halted in mid-sentence.

Alfredo's eyes went dead and his facial muscles spasmed for a single second, as if a current of electricity had shot through them, and then he relaxed, still conscious, still staring. He was apparently none the worse for it and had recovered completely. Shelley at first thought of a minor seizure or stroke, but it seemed to be neither, and a cause of progressive damage, but rather akin to a a momentary, repeated fugue state.

"This is what's been happening each time," she said, "in fifteen minute cycles. I nearly rushed down to get you, but you were so exhausted and he didn't look to be in any physical danger."

An expression of serious annoyance briefly crossed Shelley's face, but then he realised how close he was to physical collapse, and it occurred to him that, in her position, he might well have acted similarly.

"Alfredo, how are you feeling?" he said.

"Where am I? What's happened?" the boy replied.

"Don't you remember?"

"I suppose I must be in hospital. Don't remember anything after the accident. Car came at me out of nowhere. Like the Devil."

"You don't know who I am? Or remember having spoken to me before?"

"It seems to me I've only just regained consciousness. How long have I been here?"

Alfredo was perfectly lucid and entirely in command of his mental faculties, and for the next quarter of an hour, Shelley spoke with him. At that the end of that period, however, the boy had another fugue, as if his brain had been reset. The last fifteen minutes were wiped from his memory and one had to begin from scratch, explaining everything all over again.

Shelley had him sedated, since the boy was unable to fall asleep, and went back to the trolley to get some sleep himself. There was nothing more he could do for Alfredo at this stage.

Ж

The next day Shelley filled Mr. Davis in on all the details and the consultant made his own examination. The fifteen minute cycle hadn't stopped repeating, even after the sedative wore off, and showed no signs of doing so.

His aunt visited, her initial delight turning to confusion when she witnessed the phenomenon for herself.

And then there were weeks of observation.

No change at all.

Alfredo Salgado was a fully functioning human

being with a memory span confined to a short self-devouring cycle. For him, time had ground to a halt at the moment of his awakening after the accident and could advance no further than fifteen minutes before falling back to its starting point.

Davis decided eventually to operate. The inflammation had long since ceased to be a factor, and although there were dangers involved, the benefits outweighed the risks. The boy's aunt signed a consent form, by now driven half to despair, but the brain operation proved unsuccessful and there was no change to his condition. An even more radically invasive approach to deal with the issue entailed a trade-off between cognition and memory that could not be justified.

After three months Alfredo Salgado was transferred to an expensive, private mental institution just outside Highgate Village. He required constant supervision since, after a quarter of an hour, he had no idea where he was or why he had been put there. A list of written answers to his cyclical queries was hung on a plastic-coated note around his neck for his easy reference. He still could not sleep of his own volition, and required a carefully managed dose of sleeping pills each night.

His aunt visited him without fail every day, at a fixed time in the afternoon, and had almost exactly the same conversation over and over again.

CHAPTER SIX

SUSAN Huntley looked over at her husband Isaac as he watched, zombie-like, the forty-six inch plasma screen showing the blue-ray of an American comedy film whose plot development she'd started to find offensive. He would occasionally chuckle at some crass remark made by one of the characters, and even this mild sign of appreciation irritated her. They'd eaten a delicious meal of fresh pasta, courgettes, and char-grilled chicken with herbs before settling down to watch this stupid movie over a bottle of *Campo Viejo*. It was a ridiculous thing he had ordered on Ebay a week ago and which arrived in the post just this morning. He had passed no comment on the dinner at all, despite the care and attention she'd put into its preparation. He'd dutifully asked her about her day at the little boutique on the Archway Road that she ran and which sold stylish and expensive children's clothes, showed interest at all the right points in her account, but still chomped mechanically and indifferently at the food until the plate was cleared.

"This isn't funny," she said.

"No, probably not," he replied. "It's more formulaic than I thought. But it might pick up."

"Why are you chuckling then? The young women in this film are just there for middle-aged adolescents to goggle over."

Isaac didn't reply. She was right. The thing was supposedly a time-travel movie wherein a group of stock male characters change their own history. It was acutely depressing underneath all the forced jokes, retroactive winks and nods, and unfunny slapstick. He had thought it would make a change from their usual diet of B&W classic European art-cinema, Golden Age Hollywood movies with tragic female leads, or high-brow cultural documentaries, but the most angst-ridden of them was more bearable than this farrago of false optimism. Still, he thought, I bought it and so I might as well watch it to the end.

"I'm not watching anymore," Susan said. "It's making me feel sick. Lovely."

She disappeared upstairs.

Isaac Huntley poured himself another glass of wine. It was amazing that such an awful film was reproduced in quite stunning clarity. He was more hypnotised by the sharpness of the resolution provided by his top-of-the-range equipment than by any of the events unfolding on the screen. Eventually, sometime later, the film reached its conclusion; happiness for middle-aged men who'd blown their chances first time around was shown to be achievable by altering history in order to obtain gigantic, albeit unearned, material success for themselves.

He got up, took the blue-ray disc out of the player, turned off the television set, and put it back in its plastic case. He had one last glass of wine, finishing off the bottle.

The house was quiet.

Upstairs, Susan was probably reading some novel on her Kindle whilst propped up in bed and he knew tonight would be one of those occasions when she would pointedly turn away from him in the darkness rather than welcome his embrace. He would tell her she was right about the movie, but all that would do would be to affirm her sense of disappointment in his judgment.

Material success as the criterion for self-worth, the movie said. It was ironic because he, Doctor Isaac Huntley, wasn't lacking in it. He had pretty much everything he wanted in that line. An expensive old townhouse in exclusive Highgate Village, a fancy

B.M.W., an intelligent and beautiful wife, no children, an excellent pension plan and a healthy portfolio of stocks and shares. His work at the private psychiatric clinic paid extremely well, and he was very much in demand for medical conferences, with all expenses paid. If there was one thing he felt he lacked it was the wider recognition that was his due. He wanted to be known outside of his own circles for his abilities and expertise. He wanted to be admired at swank dinner parties.

There was still the case of Alfredo Salgado of course.

And tomorrow could change everything.

Ж

Susan finally turned the Kindle off. She could not concentrate properly on the dense prose of the Henry James novel she'd downloaded and the interminable clauses and sub-clauses of the author's long paragraphs required her full attention. Her mind kept turning back to Isaac's increasingly selfish behaviour. The last few months he had been distant and off-hand with her. Outwardly he kept up all the norms of consideration, complimenting her on her looks, her dress sense, enquiring about her feelings, even occasionally bringing home flowers, a thing he had not done since they had first starting living together. But there was no real warmth or enthusiasm in any of it, and the rot even extended to his mechanical, once a week, love-making; always with a condom.

He dealt with, she suspected, her own emotional requirements in the same detached professional way as he would with a patient. And yet, even this was forced. It seemed to her that he had become completely fixated by the Salgado case. Previously, he had distanced himself from it, complaining that Salgado should not be at a private clinic at all and would be much better off in an N.H.S. secure unit. Whenever he spoke of the case, she was irritated to find that it was the one subject that prompted an enthusiastic response; a feature now absent in the day-to-day of their own relationship.

Such was her distress, that she had considered going to a counsellor, and told Isaac so. It was a proposal to which he reacted with complete self-assurance and understanding, and this only made her all the more miserable. He, of course, would know exactly in advance the professional advice likely to be given her. She was not entirely sure if he guessed that she had recently reached the stage in which she had seriously considered just walking out on him. A crisis of that sort might be the only way to test his real feelings for her and shock him into realising the depths of her unhappiness.

She slipped out of bed, stood in front of the full-length mirror and looked at herself. Thirty-six years old. Her figure was slim and toned. It could have belonged to a twenty-six year old. She had always taken good care of herself, eating the right foods, regular exercise at the gym twice a week, looking after her skin meticulously. Her black hair was shiny and lustrous. She had an oval face with large, clear blue eyes that were magnetic. Rather like Bette Davis. She'd never had any difficulty attracting men. She found it hard to believe she ever would.

She heard footsteps on the stairs – Isaac coming up to the bedroom – and she slipped back into bed, turned off her bedside lamp and pretended to be asleep.

Ж

"Do you think it'll work?"

It was the following day and Dr. Isaac Huntley turned over the bottle of pills, watching the little blue contents roll around inside.

"I hope so," he finally replied to the male nurse.

The pharmacological effects of paraoxitridene were recorded in the clinical trials data as being immediate. This was a brand new drug on the market and it would be the first time he'd sanctioned its use on a patient. Once the compound entered the bloodstream (when digested with water on an empty stomach, after ten minutes) it worked on the affected region of the brain at once. Continuous mnemonic recall was re-established, provided the patient took the same dosage again at regular twenty-four hour intervals.

Still, it hadn't been tried on Alfredo Salgado. He'd been in the same cycle of disrupted memory for thirty-four years. During the last two decades it had been necessary to keep him in isolation in a room without any mirrors.

For a while in the late 1990s he had become something of a celebrity, albeit of the unwilling type who had not sought publicity in the first place but who found it sought him out. The media had dubbed him "The Time Traveller", the man who, every fifteen minutes of his life, re-awoke at 11:35pm, on October 19, 1981.

Naturally, the further the world moved away from that date, the more confusing it became to someone who had not lived through the subsequent changes. There was talk about a book being written on his case by the hack journalist whose paper first splashed the case all over its inside pages, but nothing came of it. Salgado's sole relative, his aunt Maria, refused to countenance the idea and without her cooperation the thing could have come across as sheer exploitation. Now, however …

Huntley had only worked at the Highgate Private Mental Clinic for seven years and at the start, he was amazed that Salgado wasn't confined to a straitjacket and wasn't screaming his head off every quarter of an hour.

No one had visited him now for a few weeks. The aunt had died just a month ago, worn out and half-crazy herself. Huntley had been convinced that her weekly visits had been counterproductive for a long time, since the sight of this old woman – who Salgado could have scarcely believed was still his aunt – only made him more distressed. For him, she had aged decades in a matter of a few hours.

The sole way to make Salgado's existence tolerable was to keep him both mildly sedated and on a regular course of anti-depressants and sleeping pills. He needed to be constantly monitored.

It was, Huntley thought, very much the same type of treatment as one would provide for a terminal Alzheimer's patient.

Except that Salgado was not terminal. Far from it. Given his lack of exercise he was still remarkably healthy for a forty-eight year old man. After all, he had never smoked, drunk, or over-indulged in fatty foods. A couple of his back teeth had been extracted, due to decay. And the unruly shock of thick hair on his head was pure white.

"Once I've administered the drug, come in after exactly fifteen minutes," Doctor Huntley said to the male nurse.

The man nodded.

"Well, let's give it a try," Doctor Huntley said, and he entered Salgado's room, while the male nurse waited outside.

Ж

There was nothing within to indicate what year it was. The walls were painted white, decorated only with a couple of reproductions of Van Gogh paintings; "Sunflowers" and "Starry Night". The single window looked out over the lawn behind the clinic, the view confined by a row of ferns at the far end. There was a cast iron bed with its fresh blankets and pillow, and a spotless wash basin. The well-thumbed Gideon Bible on the bedside cabinet dated from 1980. There were no mirrors. It was often difficult to get him bathed and the thing had to be done first thing in the morning, while he was still half-dozing from the sleeping pills. Rather than shaving him, it had been decided to let him have a close-cropped beard, which was easier to manage and trimmed once a week. Its salt-and-pepper colour tone contrasted sharply with his shock of totally white head hair.

Salgado's last fifteen minute cycle had completed but, just before it did, Huntley gave him the pills to swallow, and removed the laminated information card hung around his neck. It provided the patient with a brief synopsis of what had happened to him and where he was now.

There was the usual momentary tremor and then his brain reset as it always had done in the past.

"Where am I? What's happened? Why has everything shrunk in size?" he said.

"Prepare yourself for a shock Alfredo, you've been in this clinic for a long time since your accident," Huntley replied, his words so familiar to him through repetition that they came almost automatically. Salgado's reaction was just as familiar.

"What's happened to my body? What is this?" he shouted, his eyes widening with terror as he looked down at his physical form through a new pair of eye-glasses. Without sedation he would probably have been thrashing around in total panic and disorientation.

"You're safe, Alfredo, You're in no danger," Huntley said.

Salgado was running the fingers of his right hand over his face and head, obviously appalled by its strangeness to him.

"What have you DONE to me?!!" he shouted again, "Have you transplanted my brain?"

It was an accusation, so the case notes recorded, that he had been repeating since at least 1984. The fourteen year old boy gazed out in fear from behind the face of a forty-eight year old adult.

"Alfredo, you've been ill for a very long period. This is your own body. You're much older than your mind believes you are. You've been suffering from a kind of coma, think of it that way," Huntley said.

Although the doctor tried to inject some emphasis into what he was saying, the fact that he had explained all this hundreds of times before drained it of impetus. It was like speaking the same lines in a script. He was not a good enough actor to carry the attempt off, even though every word of what he said was true.

"I want to see myself in a mirror," he said. "Give me a mirror."

"I will, in a little while, later on."

Only once before had this request been complied with inside the patient's fifteen minute cycle and it had caused, unsurprisingly, an acute hysterical episode.

Salgado put a finger in his mouth and poked around inside, obviously just now noticing he had lost two back teeth.

"Am I mad?" he asked, piteously. "Tell me the truth. Is this an asylum?"

"No, you're not mad. But this is a mental health institution, a private clinic in Highgate. You've been here since 1981. It's now 2015."

"Impossible. I must be mad. Or I must be stuck in a nightmare, or else in purgatory. Where's my aunt Maria? Why isn't she here? I want to talk to her. I want a priest."

"We need to talk about your aunt later. Not now. And I'll get you a priest. But first I want you to tell me everything you remember from the beginning of the morning of the accident until right up to when the accident itself happened. In order and slowly. It's very important," Huntley said.

The doctor pretended to listen attentively and take notes on a pad of paper as Salgado began to recite the same series of events Huntley had heard countless times before. None of it was actually very important, but it was a useful distraction technique for the benefit of the patient. What really concerned Huntley was whether the drug he'd administered was going to work or not. He mentally calculated that there was only another five or so minutes to go before he found out if it had worked. If it didn't, Salgado's cycle would simply start up all over again and nothing would have been lost anyway.

In fact, it was some twenty-five minutes, not fifteen, from the moment the drug had been administered when the male nurse finally entered the room. While waiting outside he had been playing online chess on his smartphone and completely lost track of time.

Ж

"So how long has it been now?" said Adam Jones, the executive director of the Highgate Private Psychiatric Clinic.

"Two days," Huntley replied.

"No cycles at all?"

"Complete continuity. It's amazing."

The two men were sitting in Jones' office.

"This throws up a whole new series of considerations," Jones said.

"I realise that. For one thing he's entirely lucid, and our first priority should be to assist his gradual re-integration into society. However, although legally he's an adult, he's mentally a fourteen year old, even though he's quite the most intellectually precocious fourteen year old imaginable, but now one with the physical brain and body of a forty-eight year old."

"Yes, I get that."

"This is quite aside from the problem of adjustment from someone whose only points of reference are from 1981 or earlier and who knows nothing of all the changes in the world that have taken place since that date. I don't see how he can function outside in the community without months of gradual preparation."

"What does he want to do?" Jones said.

"He wants to get out of here as soon as possible, and I don't blame him. I had to tell him his aunt's dead. He took it badly."

"He's her sole beneficiary. Legally, he's of an age to inherit it all once he's out of here. We can scarcely apply to have him sectioned. Difficult. He came into our clinic in eighty-one as a minor."

"Presumably some firm of solicitors is administering his aunt's estate?"

"That's right. Lindop and Crawford. Came in a couple of weeks ago. Seedy offices above a shop up on the High Street. Been there for decades. The only reason Salgado wasn't immediately transferred to an N.H.S. clinic when the aunt died – oh, a month back – was that there was proviso in the will for Salgado's continued treatment here. They've put the house up on the market to pay for it."

"What do you think?" Huntley said.

"I don't see how we can keep him here forcibly, certainly not without it turning ugly and causing some kind of scandal that might end up in the courts or, even worse, the papers."

"Hmmm …" Huntley replied.

The idea of writing a book himself on the case rose up into the forefront of his mind once more.

Ж

"I'm telling you again, quite reasonably, that you have no grounds for keeping me here," Salgado said.

It was day three after the drug had first been administered. Salgado's memory remained unbroken, and, provided he took it every twenty four hours, it looked as if no further severe episodes might occur. Huntley doubted that there would be any complete falling back into the earlier state. His best guess was that there might be isolated examples of mild memory loss. Yet even these might not arise if the dosage was correctly increased as tolerance to it rose. Moreover, it was pretty clear from the clinical trials that any such individual patient tolerance to the drug was only likely to develop in the body after several months of treatment. Really, it was next to impossible to justify keeping Salgado locked up in his room solely on medical grounds.

"How are you sleeping?" he said.

"I am doing so without the soporific pills," Salgado replied. "Since last night."

"You didn't take them?"

"I didn't need them. I'm exhausted from all this prisoner nonsense. It was actually a relief to lose consciousness. Don't you realise how boring it is to be shut up in here with nothing to do all day except read that vulgar Protestant bible and stare at a couple of Van Gogh paintings? I almost think you are trying to drive me insane so you can keep me here."

Huntley chuckled.

"What would you do if you were free to leave today?" the doctor asked him.

"I assume I still have access to my late, dear aunt's house. Moreover, I also assume I have enough money left by her to me in order for me to resume my life upon whatever basis I choose to do so. Most of all I wish to get back to my private research into scholasticism."

"Despite that, you've never lived alone and had to look after yourself. In terms of life experience you're still a fourteen year old boy. I am not sure you're capable of managing your own financial affairs. That's got to be a consideration. Secondly, and perhaps even more worth thinking about, you have no idea what the world of 2015 is like compared to 1981."

"I don't care if people ferry themselves around now with personal jet-packs, have robots cook their meals and if most of them have moved to Mars after a Third World War with the Soviet Union. You have no right to keep me here. Unless you let me out today I will sue you. You know that tomorrow my aunt's solicitor Mr. Harold Lindop is coming here to visit me. You will be charged with kidnapping or false imprisonment."

"That won't be necessary. You're right. We can't keep you here without your consent. I had hoped to persuade you it was the best thing. But obviously not," Huntley said, resigned to the inevitable.

He took out some keys and an envelope containing two hundred pounds in banknotes from his pocket.

"These are for your aunt's house," he said. "Lindop's clerk dropped them over earlier today. He asked me to tell you that Lindop will visit you there tomorrow to discuss your affairs. At three thirty in the afternoon."

He passed the house keys and the envelope over to Salgado.

"I'd like to visit you a couple of times a week to see how you're getting on, would that be possible?" Huntley said. "Though you won't remember it, I have actually known you for quite a long period now. You'll also need these. Take one a day without fail. I can't be held responsible for the consequences if you come off the drug."

He gave Salgado a small bottle of blue pills, a month's supply of paraoxitridene.

CHAPTER SEVEN

ALFREDO Salgado, having left the Highgate Clinic, found himself not only in an alien body but also in a shrunken alien world. He could not shake off the conviction that he had somehow become trapped in an outlandish lucid dream from which it was impossible to awaken.

He doubted he would ever recover from the shock of learning so suddenly that his aunt Maria was dead. His grief was enormous. He now had no protector, no guiding light, no other relative to help him. He was utterly alone in the world and knew that the house he was going back to would be empty without her and probably substantially altered. Had she thrown out his private library? What of his notebooks on Scholasticism? Did they remain? Perhaps she had kept them stored, knowing how much he valued them, in the hopeful expectation of his final recovery – the miraculous recovery she, alas, did not live to witness. During the last three days he had to adjust himself to occupying what was, to his mind, the body of an old man. He had noted with curiosity the way the people in the clinic had interacted with him. His physical form lent his demands and arguments a gravitas that he had not experienced before. He could tell that no one was certain whether his mental or chronological age was the determining factor in the way they should respond to him. And Alfredo quickly grasped how necessary it was to gaining his liberty that he call upon every last aspect of precociousness he possessed. Without it, he had no doubt he would still be a prisoner, if not at the clinic, then at some N.H.S. mental ward. But even though the bluff had paid off, nothing could have prepared him for what he found as he made his way up North Hill towards Highgate Village.

The first thing he noticed was how all the motor vehicles had changed shape, from box-like angular to soft curved lines, and, despite the greater numbers of them, how much less noisy they were. So, too, how much less litter there was on the pavements and the complete absence of dog muck. Everything seemed to be in much better repair, buildings, pavements and shop fronts. It was as if the whole region had been refurbished and gentrified overnight.

The streetlamps were completely different, much higher up and modern, the old ornate ones torn down and replaced.

And the sturdy red phone boxes too seemed to have almost disappeared. A few drab grey and functional replacements remained – invariably unused.

He saw a bus stop, and was surprised to see people milling around it, not forming a proper queue, and he decided to mingle with them for a few minutes to observe their behaviour. Fully half of them were staring, zombie-like, at the glowing screens of hand-held devices – about the size of a pocket electronic calculator – or else were talking into them, holding conversations. Inside the bus shelter was a dot matrix display, showing the bus arrival times. The display was in English, but Alfredo also noted, with surprise, that half the conversations the people were holding were not in English at all, but in a variety of foreign languages and accents – even some from the Eastern European Communist Bloc.

He remained there until a bus turned up. It was not one of the familiar Routemasters, but a driver-only operated single-decker. No one paid a cash fare as they clambered aboard the vehicle, but each person's entry was logged electronically with a beep from a kind of plastic travel card they carried.

For some reason, eight of ten people seemed to be

dressed in black, as if it were a civilian uniform, like that of the Mosleyites in the 1930s or as if they were on their way to a funeral. And, for some other reason, very few people appeared to be smoking. There were hardly any cigarette butts littering the pavement around the bus shelter, as had been commonplace before.

He wandered away from the stop and further up North Hill until he passed Highgate School, which scarcely seemed to have altered at all. Ahead was a pub with a mock-Tudor frontage called "The Gatehouse", and he suddenly decided to go inside and make his first visit to one of those hostelries. He had never been allowed inside a pub before, and it would be a useful occasion, he imagined, not only to establish his sudden ascension to full adulthood, but to familiarise himself with the people of 2015. He recalled, too, that his great literary hero Sinclair Egremont Xavier, the Catholic author and philosopher, had written a great deal about the beneficial social aspects of tavern life and consuming traditional English ale in vast quantities. He envisaged it would have as pleasurable an effect as the glass of *Rioja* his aunt used to give him after Sunday luncheon.

He paused at the threshold before entering however, as a particular thought had now occurred to him. But, looking over the label on the small bottle of pills, he saw nothing therein to indicate he should avoid alcohol.

Ж

The place was not particularly busy, and no one took any notice of Alfredo as he entered. Whenever he had looked through the windows of pubs in the past, their patrons existed in a permanent fog of tobacco smoke. But here no one at all indulged in pipes or cigarettes. It appeared to be voluntary behaviour, since there were no signs dotted around the place stating that no smoking was allowed.

Moving in from the doorway he was suddenly dazzled by a large flat-screen television – with an incredibly sharp detailed picture and highly vivid colours – at the far end of the curved bar counter. It seemed to be showing a news programme of some type, and a continuous strip of information rolled across the bottom of the screen.

Having been forced to read George Orwell's book *Nineteen Eighty-Four* (which he found philosophically illiterate, atheist and absurd) during English lessons, he now recalled how the televisions in that novel had been two-way devices which not only broadcast to, but also monitored, the venues wherein they were sited. If the newsreaders on the programme were actually observing the pub then at least the populace had some freedom from interference; for the sound was turned off.

The barman had wandered along the counter to serve Alfredo, who was now looking over the range of traditional ales on tap and trying to make his mind up as to which he should sample. He settled on something called "Titanic", simply because he liked the design of the label attached to the pump handle.

"One of those please," Alfredo said, pointing to it. The unfamiliar sound of his own voice still surprised him. It was always deeper than he expected, and seemed to issue from some region far further down his throat than previously.

"Pint or half?" replied the barman.

" … ermm, pint I think," Alfredo replied.

The barman pulled the pint and put the straight glass of foaming ale on the counter. Alfredo thought beer was served in squat glass tankards with handles.

"Three pounds eighty," said the barman.

Alfredo was inwardly astonished. The rate of inflation must be astronomical in this future world, or else ale was now a luxury item like champagne. He rummaged around in the pocket of his overcoat and pulled out the envelope containing the two hundred pounds he had been given. The amount was scarcely the small fortune he had imagined it to be. As he struggled with the unfamiliar notes (all of which seemed to have shrunk in size), an elderly man in his mid to late sixties standing alongside him at the bar counter waiting to be served stared intently at the sight of the money.

"Do what wilt shall be the whole of the law. Hey, don't I know you?" the stranger said, his voice slightly slurred by drink and with a thick Cockney accent.

Alfredo looked him over.

The stranger was wearing a very shabby grey raincoat with the collar turned up, a pair of old jeans and what looked like running shoes. His thin, horsey face was extremely pale and lined with creases. Dirty grey hair was plastered across his forehead. He was missing two teeth from the front of his lower jaw. In his left hand he carried an orange Sainsburys plastic bag full of pamphlets.

Alfredo had no idea who the stranger was. He shook his head by way of reply.

"You were in the papers weren't you? About 1998 I think it was. Waking coma or something. Spanish name," the stranger said, persisting in his queries.

Alfredo wasn't particularly keen on socialising with this individual, but decided that he had to begin somewhere, and with someone, in trying to familiarise himself with the age.

He handed over a ten pound note to the barman.

"Very kind of you to offer, just a double Jamesons for me," the stranger said.

The barman looked at Alfredo as if he had seen this trick a thousand times before, but Alfredo nodded assent, and the barman produced the drink after entering the transaction on a touch-screen cash register. Alfredo pocketed the unfamiliar change. Pound notes seemed to have been phased out altogether.

"I guess you don't mind my joining you," the stranger said, leading him towards a secluded, vacant booth on the far side of the bar where they sat down facing one another. "Let me introduce myself – I'm Dorian Marsh. Perhaps you've heard of me. I too have been in the papers in my time, being a specialist in investigating occult occurrences."

"I'm Alfredo Salgado," he replied. "Pleased to meet you."

"Likewise. Well, cheers," Marsh said, as he took a long gulp at his whiskey.

Alfredo took his first sip of traditional ale. He could taste hops on his tongue and, although it wasn't exactly unpleasant, he was somewhat disappointed. He wondered why Sinclair Egremont Xavier had extolled the virtues of ale so highly. It did not compare to the taste of *Rioja*.

Ж

An hour later, after three more pints of the increasingly invigorating "Titanic", Alfredo found that he was enjoying himself enormously. He felt quite light-headed, and noticed how talkative he was.

This person Dorian Marsh, whose drinks Alfredo now happily insisted on paying for, was proving a mine of fascinating information. He advised Alfredo that the modern world was currently being run by a secret cabal called "The Magisteriarti" who controlled the media and the governments of the world.

"They even engineered the fall of the Berlin Wall back in 1990," Marsh said.

"Surely that would have led to a Soviet invasion of Western Europe," Alfredo replied.

Marsh had never met anyone who knew so little about modern history. Surely Salgado couldn't have been in a coma until only very recently? He was trying to recall the medical details of the newspaper article about him he'd read years ago in 1998, but it was a fuzzy memory. Perhaps Salgado was simply pulling his leg. He certainly seemed to be getting drunk quickly and obviously wasn't used to strong ale. Anyway, he was generous with his money, which was the main thing. Marsh's measly two-weekly state pension payment wasn't going to be in his bank account for another three days yet, and he was sick of drinking cheap lager in his one bedroom cellar flat. He hadn't sold any of his self-published pamphlets about his investigations into the occult for weeks.

"There hasn't been a Soviet Union for decades. It collapsed and was split up. Communism fell. It was an obstacle to the further worldwide financial and political rule of The Magisteriarti. It had served its purpose and was no longer useful."

"It seems to me that the fall of communism could scarcely be other than a cause for celebration," Alfredo said.

"Don't get me wrong, I'm not a communist. I'm not even political. Politics has been abolished now anyway. There's only one world government and it operates secretly. Its goal is to control everyone else and maintain an occult dynasty based on wealth, sex magic and influence."

Alfredo was having trouble following all of this. There were inherent contradictions in what Marsh was claiming, but perhaps it was not the case that what he said was untrue, but rather that he was not much of a logician.

"Well," said Alfredo, "if people are aware of this conspiracy, and speak as you do, freely, there must be some organised resistance to it."

He recalled again George Orwell's novel *Nineteen Eighty-Four* in which the ideology was enforced not only by propaganda but also by rigorous police state brutality. This society didn't seem to be operating on that model, or at least not openly and visibly.

"Most people are too stupid to notice it," Marsh said. "And a lot of them even like it. They think Facebook, Instagram and Twitter are a good way of keeping up with everyone and making new contacts."

Alfredo had no idea what the terms meant and his face expressed bemusement.

"Look," Marsh went on, "there's some resistance on the internet, it's true. My own website gets dozens of hits everyday for a start. Have you seen it?"

"I don't know what all those things are. Are they new television programmes? Do you work for I.T.V. or perhaps the Open University?" Alfredo said, noticing that the ale had affected his judgement. Without its faculty of engendering a sense of gregariousness in its imbibers, he doubted that he would have stood much more of the gibberish Marsh was spouting.

"What are you on about? I can't help thinking you're having a laugh, but here …" Marsh said, taking one of the hand-held devices out of his pocket that everyone appeared to have in their possession.

He touched the screen a few times and slid the thing across the table for Alfredo to look at.

"Have a read of that. I'm going outside for a smoke," he said, producing a pouch of tobacco and some papers and quickly hand-rolling a cigarette. "Lend me a tenner will you and I'll get a round in on the way back?"

Alfredo nodded absently and handed over a twenty without looking at it.

While Marsh was outside smoking Alfredo examined the text. He rapidly got the hang of navigating through the various pages of Marsh's written works and embedded photographs and layouts. It was astonishing to him that such a vast amount of data could all be contained within this one tiny machine.

He recalled the so-called Computer Department at Southwood School, in which a noisy machine had occupied half a room, with a terminal that generated reams of print-off paper. There were a few advanced personal home computers he'd seen – aside from the idiotic and expensive games machines that ran things like ping-pong – such as the Sinclair ZX80, but as far as he could recall they could scarcely be used for anything practical, aside from number crunching, and ownership of one of them amounted to a status symbol for those sad materialists obsessed with technology at the expense of their souls.

Not that Marsh had employed the vastly increased potential of this new device for anything useful. His written works were a sorry collection of madcap and half-illiterate gibberish, the sort of private ramblings that paranoid-schizophrenics used to scribble in notepads on yellow paper. Even with the general air of bonhomie and decreased degree of critical acumen Alfredo noticed was a side-effect of ale-drinking, he could not prevent himself chuckling over the absurdity of Marsh's writings.

The first page he encountered was concerned with what was termed "The Uncanny Vortex of Crouch End". It listed, amongst other things, all the 1970s and 1980s horror fiction authors (with one or two "famous" Americans included who Salgado had never heard of) who had lived either in the region or on the borders, some fairly recent English zombie movie that had been filmed on Weston Park, a well-publicised urban legend of a King Vampire being staked in a now burnt-down Neo-Gothic house on Crescent Road thirty years ago, an account of a poltergeist in Ferrestone Road dating from 1921, and contemporary reports of ghost trains and creepy goblins spotted on the disused, overgrown Northern Heights branch line from Finsbury Park to Alexandra Park.

Looking over some of the other pages that were not devoted to local north London legends, hauntings and the like, Salgado realised Marsh's main gripe with the omnipotent, so-called "Magisteriati" appeared to be that he himself hadn't been admitted into the ranks of its powerful elite.

When he noticed Marsh making his way back with the refills of ale and whiskey he stifled his laughter and assumed a straight face.

"Pretty impressive, huh?" Marsh said, sitting down. There didn't seem to be any change forthcoming from the twenty-pound note. Perhaps inflation had increased the prices – even during the relatively short span of time that they'd both been drinking.

"I can see why you would want to keep this information secret and recorded only on your device," Alfredo said.

"My blog's not set to private, anyone can read it. That's the whole point."

"Are you saying that anyone who owns one of these devices can see your writings?"

"Look, have you just come out of that coma – or whatever it was – in the last half hour? Of course anyone can read it, they don't need a smartphone. They can see it on their laptops, their i-Pads or whatever. Don't you even know what the internet is?"

Marsh then pushed more symbols on the screen and showed Alfredo a variety of websites, some containing what looked like endless private television channels that were each run by individual persons, an encyclopedia whose scope was mind-numbingly diffuse and incredibly shallow, and finally something truly diabolical that consisted of a wall of pictures of people's faces alongside a stream of inane gossip and mindless chatter. Jammed in-between it all was a parade of annoying advertising. It was like an infinite tabloid newspaper that interacted with its readers to keep their attention at the level of the lowest common denominator.

"And everyone has access to this internet thing?" Alfredo said, aghast at the spectacle.

"Of course they do. Except in parts of places like Africa or other poor countries where they're deprived and starved of data."

Alfredo's head swam. All the internet information wasn't contained on the devices themselves. They only accessed it, as with a broadcast signal. People who indulged regularly in this vast dimension of internet were in danger of permanently damaging their capacity to reason; in the much same way as people had who did nothing but sit staring vacantly at the television every evening. Still, presumably he had seen only a very small fraction of it. Perhaps it wasn't all like that.

"What about real books? Doesn't anyone read books any longer?"

For some reason his voice had become slurred.

"The bookshops are mostly closing down. There aren't many left. Haven't been for the last ten years. No one uses them. Even the libraries are going digital. You can read nearly any book online now anyway. And people can publish their own books without official or corporate interference. Hang on a minute, someone's left a message on my blog that needs a reply."

Marsh began pushing with his thumb at the screen, on which had appeared a miniature typewriter keyboard. He was thoroughly engrossed in the activity.

As he did so Alfredo again wondered about the fate of his collection of books. Had his aunt sold them off long ago, seeing them as redundant and space-consuming what with the advent of the modern internet zone? His dear *tia* had never been a scholar herself, hated clutter, and Alfredo felt she erred somewhat too much on the side of fideism. For his own part he felt a book (or at least one that was not a fictional, poetical or technical work) lacked proper authority unless it contained the *nihil obstat* and *imprimatur* declaring it free from heresy. False modernist ideas were all too often presented as self-evident, when they were invariably self-contradictory, and without having any grounding in logically demonstrable first principles.

Alfredo suddenly yawned loudly. It was not a voluntary action and he was amazed at himself and his lack of decorum. He felt incredibly tired. He was finding it hard to keep his eyes open. His tongue felt thick and too large for his mouth.

Marsh had finished with his typing and tapped the side of his empty whiskey glass.

"Shall we get one more for the road?" he said.

Alfredo nodded, his head tipping forward further than he wanted it to. Something was wrong with his sense of balance. He absent-mindedly slid the envelope containing the bank notes over the table for Marsh to remove enough for another round of drinks.

While Marsh was up at the counter getting served, Alfredo's head tipped forward again and he passed out, half-slumped across the table.

Ж

"Closing time," a voice said loudly in his ear.

Someone was shaking his shoulder insistently.

"Come on, closing time. Off you go," the voice went on.

Alfredo raised his head from the table-top. All the lights in the place had been dimmed, the customers were gone and the barman was standing over him, a dull look of impatience on his face.

"Where's Dorian Marsh?" Alfredo said, groggily.

"He left straight after drinking up last orders half an hour ago," the barman said.

Alfredo clambered to his feet. His mind was still slightly disordered from the "Titanic" ale, but he was confident he could make his way back to his late aunt's house on Causton Road. It was all downhill and he remembered the route.

On the porch entranceway outside the Gatehouse Tavern Alfredo paused unsteadily on his feet as the barman locked the door for the night.

The pockets of his coat were bulging. He discovered he had somehow acquired several of Marsh's pamphlets. And there was only forty pounds left in his envelope of cash.

A sense of profound fear bubbled up from the depths of his mind, and he felt like the thing he was, a confused fourteen year old boy; which realisation had successfully been kept at bay until that moment. The effect of the ale prevented the fear from overwhelming him, but he was aware that he very much disliked the idea of walking the streets alone at night and of returning to the now-empty house he had once shared with his aunt. But he muttered an *Ave Maria* and a *Pater Noster* under his breath and set off.

He crossed the street and skirted the centre of Highgate Village. The shops were almost all completely unfamiliar. A large proportion of them seemed to house estate-agents. Again he noticed that the mix of early and late Georgian architecture hadn't changed and the majority of the buildings, streets and pavements (as with those on North Hill) looked better maintained than they had been thirty-odd years ago. There were certainly more people around at this time of night, he noticed, and more road traffic.

He turned left down Southwood Lane, intending to pass his school, but when he reached the right location he found the old building had been replaced by a small estate of two-storey houses that had been erected on the site twenty years ago. The shock of the school's – from his perspective – almost overnight disappearance and replacement made him pause for several moments, trying to take it in. He wondered what had happened to all the pupils and teachers during the intervening years – those people who, to Alfredo, were more real than any of the pedestrians now passing in the shadows of the strange new world.

Archway Road, too, was even busier than he expected. The motor vehicle traffic at this hour, just short of midnight, was as frequent as a weekend afternoon in 1981. The thing seemed incomprehensible. Was there an epidemic of insomnia?

Alfredo drifted down the hill, pausing again opposite the vast Gothic-style bulk of Jackson's Lane Community Centre – next to the crossing where he had been the victim of the hit-and-run driver who was the cause of everything that had happened to him since. During the whole turmoil of the last three days he had not thought to ask Doctor Huntley whether the

145

perpetrator had ever been caught. Perhaps there had been an epidemic of such incidents too, for the few seconds when pedestrians could safely cross the road were signalled by a deafening electronic racket as the traffic lights changed to red.

Slightly further on Alfredo saw a shop open that sold a variety of goods. It resembled a green grocers store, except that it also sold alcohol, like an off-licence. He slipped inside, a little startled when the door beeped behind him to denote his entry. It was probably a highly expensive outlet, since it was amazingly well-maintained, and even had a small colour television screen behind the counter recording what went on in the store. He moved along the aisle and found a cold cabinet containing a variety of tinned beer. He picked up four cans of Guinness and then a packet of Ginger-Nut biscuits from the shelves on the other side.

The Guinness, he thought, would make him sleepy again and force the fear back. Strange how when one consumed beer there seemed no end to the desire for more.

The grumpy man at the counter, who appeared to be from the far East, wasn't very communicative and only nodded absently in reply to Alfredo's greeting.

"Good evening, I'm surprised and relieved you're open so late."

As the man put his purchases in a plastic bag,

Alfredo glanced around him. There was a huge carved pumpkin on the shelf behind the counter and a series of masks for sale depicting ghosts, goblins, witches and the like. A banner draped above them declared "Happy Halloween".

Aside from the odd ridiculous horror film shown late at night on I.T.V. on All-Souls Eve, Alfredo recalled nothing of this "festival", certainly not when compared to the much more popular anti-Catholic frenzy of "Guy Fawkes Night" when scruffy children wheeled sinister stuffed dummies around the streets and begged for small change. It seemed that Druidic paganism had either returned to England or else the Americans had imposed, *in toto*, godless customs on the country. Perhaps he might expect an outbreak of enthusiasm for "Thanksgiving Day" in a few weeks.

"Six Pounds fifty," the man said.

That still left him with over thirty pounds. And the solicitor Mr. Lindop was coming by tomorrow, doubtless to give him more money anyway.

Alfredo had never tried cigarettes, and, from what he could tell, they were now regarded as worthless because they were all kept behind a sliding opaque screen and not displayed for sale. There were electronic versions of them on display instead. They appeared to use liquid tobacco instead of rolled tobacco leaves. He supposed they were now the more fashionable choice

147

for adults and were designed like pipes, but without a bowl.

It would certainly be to his advantage to appear as adult as possible when meeting with Mr. Lindop.

"Oh and one of these electric cigarette-pipes," Alfredo said, dropping a starter kit into the bag.

"Twenty Six Pounds fifty," the man said.

Alfredo paid him and left the shop.

Ж

He experienced no difficulty in locating his old home, though, as ever, he was amazed at how it appeared to have shrunk in size. He almost had the urge to crouch as he let himself in through the front door and into the hallway and turned on the light-switch.

Some of the furniture had changed, and all of the wallpaper, but the smell was just the same. He still half-expected his aunt to come out of the back-depths to greet him with a kiss on the cheek.

Settling himself on the sofa in the parlour, after removing a dust sheet, he opened one of the tins of beer. It fizzed and spewed a fifth of its contents, as if the fluid were contained under pressure, and he poured the rest into a glass from the wall-side cabinet. As he drank the rest he noticed his aunt's collection of vinyl classical records had disappeared, replaced by little silver discs in boxes that seemed to serve the same purpose. He couldn't find the machine designed to play any of them, however, at least in the parlour. There was a device connected to one of those new flat-screen televisions, but he doubted that was the right one. Anyway, he couldn't figure out how to open the top up and insert one of the discs.

Eventually, he ate the packet of Ginger-Nut biscuits, kicked off his shoes and fell asleep on the sofa.

CHAPTER EIGHT

ALFREDO awoke just after noon the next day. The first thing he was aware of was he felt quite ill. The second was that he was still dressed in the same clothes. His throat was parched, his lips caked with debris, and he had a terrible headache. His clothes clung to his skin unpleasantly and smelt of the beer-soaking from the night before.

He rolled off of the sofa and went into the kitchen, drinking water directly from the tap over the sink. Once his thirst had eased, he put his head under the steady flow, trying to wash away the miasma that clouded his thoughts.

Of course he wasn't, he realised, actually ill at all, at least in the sense of having a cold, the measles or chicken pox. He'd read about "hangovers" somewhere, though not from the work of Sinclair Egremont Xavier,

151

who had been strangely silent on the subject, in amongst his frequent paeans in praise of ale and wine.

Alfredo resolved to bring the matter to Father Laker's attention when he went to confession later that day at the Chapel of Pope St. Zosimus. There could be no question other than that severe drunkenness was a sin requiring absolution. And anyway he had a lot to talk over with the priest.

In one of the kitchen cupboards he found some aspirin and took a tablet along with his daily dose of the drug Huntley had prescribed and which he took from the little plastic bottle in his coat pocket. He had not, at first, found the container. It had been lurking inside a scrunched-up copy of one of Marsh's occult booklets.

Mr. Lindop, the solicitor, was, Alfredo recalled, scheduled to arrive at around three-thirty. He, or one of his employees, must have already been into the house the day before since there were some food supplies laid out, eggs and milk in the fridge, and cereal and crackers on the kitchen table. Alfredo ate a late breakfast, trusting only the milk and cereal, since he didn't quite know how to cook eggs, and noticed the pain behind his eyes soften as the aspirin began to dissolve in his stomach and work its way into his bloodstream.

He wanted to change his apparel but realised at once that even were there any of his old clothes left in the house they'd not only all be the wrong size for him but also look ridiculous to wear at his age. Aunt Maria must have thrown them out long ago. The thought made him start and impelled the association; what of his precious library and his notebooks? What fate had they suffered in the thirty odd years he had been absent from the world?

Although he initially flew from the breakfast table with the easy impetuousness of a lithe teenager, he was groping at the bannister rail on the third flight of stairs like an unfit middle-aged man. Physical age and the hangover had slowed him down so that he was puffing as he pushed open the door into his old attic room.

Nothing had changed within, except for the (increasingly common) illusion that everything had shrunk in size. His theological and philosophical books were all in place, meticulously ordered alphabetically across several glass cases and on covered shelves arranged around the walls of the room. The little school-desk where he worked at his private studies still reposed in front of the window under the eaves with its view over the jumble of surrounding rooftops and chimney stacks. In the old trunk next to his bed (now far too small for him to occupy) he found all of his notebooks intact and preserved, only the yellowing of the pages indicating the passage of decades since he'd seen them last.

He knelt down in front of the familiar huge black crucifix mounted on the wall opposite the door and mouthed a prayer of thanks to Christ Jesus, and then to his Aunt Maria for her steadfastness to him, adding a prayer that her time in purgatory be brief.

After he'd finished he got to his feet again, looking around the attic room. The school-desk and the bed would have to be thrown away and, so too, all the schoolboy clothes in the wardrobe that his aunt had also retained in memory of him. None of them were of any use. Gradually, he thought, he could expand his library across the confines of the house, throw out all the extraneous contents, and turn it into a distinguished, private, religious scholar's retreat with theological books on each floor.

Ж

"Well, I think that's about everything," said Mr. Lindop.

The elderly solicitor had spent the past hour going over the details of Alfredo's affairs, which tedious information Alfredo had tried to absorb as best he could. During the discussion Alfredo had puffed away sagely on the electric cigarette-pipe he had eventually managed to operate and, though the vapour made him a little light-headed, the effect was far from unpleasant. His hangover had almost disappeared and when he offered Mr. Lindop a glass of Guinness from the supply of cans left over from the night before, the solicitor appeared suitably impressed by Alfredo's adult nonchalance – even when it came to his smelly beer-stained clothes. Lindop was a man in his late sixties, of tremendous experience with all types of client, and radiated an aura of absolute discretion and self-confidence.

The white-haired solicitor told him that he would enjoy a life annuity of forty thousand pounds thanks to his late aunt's insurance policies and investments, and that, moreover, the mortgage on the house (which was now his property entirely) had been paid off last year. Alfredo had no need to work for a living and, provided he was frugal, would be without money concerns indefinitely. Lindop had set up a bank account, which papers of authorisation Alfredo signed during their discussion, and gave him a bank card to withdraw funds and pay for goods.

The bank card had caused some confusion since Alfredo had expected cash, or a cheque book, and it took a little time before he could be made to understand how ubiquitous the little plastic cards with a microchip now were in contemporary society.

Ж

Just before five o'clock Alfredo set off for the Chapel of
Pope St. Zosimus to make his confession.

It was only a short walk from the house in Causton
Road to the little backstreet on Orchard Road where the
chapel was located in amongst a series of nondescript
terraced houses. Alfredo regretted that he had not been
able to change into clean-smelling clothes for the
occasion, but since he had none, he thought he might
well be able to loan some from Father Laker, for they
were now approximately the same size and build. He
was aware that the priest would be more than thirty
years older than before, probably well into his seventies,
although Alfredo had never been entirely clear as to
exactly how old Laker had been in 1981. Back then
anyone out of their teens had seemed to him to be quite
aged. It was only due to the fact that, for Alfredo,
scarcely a few days had passed from 1981 to 2015, that
he did not consider the real possibility of the priest
having been replaced by a younger man or even of his
having died.

Again, Alfredo was struck by the change in the
area he knew so well and whose streets he had walked
so often. The new cars on the road were mostly spotless,
almost silent, and with invisible emissions, whereas
before many of the vehicles were battered wrecks, their
engines much louder, trailing clouds of thick black
exhaust fumes. So, too, previously pavements were

often cracked, poorly maintained and hazardous with dog mess, with litter strewn in the gutters, whereas now they were all carefully maintained and free of debris. Even fallen leaves were apparently swiftly removed from the streets.

Nothing, it appeared, could be allowed to fall into disuse any more. Every house was occupied. The Dorchester Tavern, on the corner of Northwood Road, though empty and closed, was being renovated, with evidence of building work going on inside. It seemed so recently that he had passed it by, glancing sheepishly through the windows, when it was alive and full to bursting with Irish drinkers in cloth caps, knocking back pints and glasses of whiskey, all with a cigarette dangling from their lips, and a mist of tobacco smoke drifting endlessly around the ornate Victorian interior.

As Alfredo reached the corner of Orchard Road he noticed an entrance on the bank next to the arched bridge over which the old abandoned railway line had run. His aunt had warned him about exploring in that area, since it had become a local dumping ground for junk and was overrun with rats. His schoolmates had told lurid tales about what they'd seen there, and he recalled Dorian Marsh's citing an urban legend about ghost trains in one of his ridiculous pamphlets. The line, it appeared, judging by the notice at the entrance, had been cleared into a parkland nature walk, and although

Alfredo was tempted to take a look, he deferred doing so, since it was getting dark and, in any case, he had to go to confession.

Halfway up Orchard Road, where the Chapel of Pope St. Zosimus should have been, there was instead a square modern block three floors in height standing in its place. For a moment he thought he had made a mistake, but after wandering up and down a little way along the street in both directions, until he stood outside it again, he ruled out the possibility. Unlike the chapel building the replacement structure was not set back from the terraced houses but on the same level as them. A sign outside the front read "Orchard Sheltered Housing: Haringey Council Healthcare."

He considered the matter for a brief while and then pushed the buzzer marked "caretaker/supervisor" on a board next to a glass-door entrance. After a delay of ten seconds a person stealthily emerged into the unlit hallway beyond. The person peered at Alfredo quizzically. Realising that he wasn't intending to leave without being spoken to, the person finally advanced to the door and opened it very slightly.

"Visiting hours are over," the person said.

Alfredo could not determine whether it was a male or female. Even the voice was of an indeterminate nature. The person's hair was cropped short and Alfredo could detect no sign of any specific gender one way or the other. He or she was wholly androgynous, and wearing some kind of loose baggy tracksuit.

"Pardon me, umm … Sir … umm … Madam … umm … for bothering you," Alfredo said.

"Are you drunk?" the person said, sniffing the air suspiciously.

"No, not at all. I'm actually looking for Father Laker," Alfredo said. "The Chapel of Pope St. Zosimus? Are you at all familiar with … "

"That burnt down years ago," the person cut in, "try up at St. Jerome's. They'll know. The big Catholic Church with the green dome on Highgate Hill. Goodbye."

Ж

Ten minutes later Alfredo was kneeling in a confessional box inside the vast expanse of St. Jerome's. He was the last of the penitents to arrive.

It was his intention to ask the priest about Father Laker and the Chapel of Pope St. Zosimus after he had made his confession, been absolved and made an act of contrition for his sin of gluttony in the form of drunkenness.

"Bless me Father for I have sinned," Alfredo began. Then he paused. The next part was awkward.

"When was your last confession?" the priest

replied. His voice sounded very familiar even though slightly muffled by the dividing wall and the lattice-work of the grille that separated them.

"Strictly speaking, thirty-four years ago," Alfredo said, still wondering why he seemed to recognise the voice.

He thought he heard the priest mutter something unintelligible to himself under his breath, like a stifled rebuke.

"Well, the important thing is that you've finally sought absolution," the priest eventually said, as if reminding himself his spiritual role was to cure as much as to judge.

"When I said strictly, I actually meant chronologically, Father. For me, my last confession wasn't more than a week ago."

"So which is it?" the priest said, a note of slight annoyance creeping into his voice.

Alfredo then explained his exact circumstances. During the process of the explanation, the priest made a series of extremely startling noises – yelps and gulps – quite out of keeping with the reserve and decorum that Alfredo would have expected from his confessor.

Finally, however, he confessed his sin of last night, and the priest muttered the words of absolution as one might ask someone to pass the sugar at tea.

As an act of contrition Alfredo was asked to say

three "Our Fathers" and three "Hail Marys", which he found an extremely lenient penance. However, he had no way of telling to what extent deviation from sound doctrine had further taken hold in the church since 1981.

He consoled himself instead with the orthodox certainty that it is in the office of the priest, and not in the conduct of the individual person, that sacramental apostolic powers are vested.

"I want to ask you something else, Father," Alfredo said. "It's about a person called Father Laker. I don't know if you are familiar with his name."

The priest now actually groaned aloud.

"Very well," he finally said. "Give me a moment."

Alfredo left the confessional box and sat down on one of the pews nearby.

Ten seconds later the priest to whom Alfredo had made his confession emerged from the box, and it was a familiar figure who made his way across the aisle and sat beside him.

Alfredo was astonished.

Although he had obviously aged dramatically, there was no mistaking the identity of the priest. He even possessed the same old Trotsky goatee-beard (though now all snow-white), though he had become quite bald on top; and it was, in fact, Alfredo's old History teacher from Southwood School – Dennis

Spencer.

"Hello Alfredo," he said, with a strange, forced smile on his face. "I imagine it is as much of a surprise for you to see me here as it is for me to see you again."

At first Alfredo could not believe the evidence of his own senses.

The power of speech seemed to have deserted him and he stared at Father Spencer silently, only his wide-open, unblinking eyes and mouth betraying the profound sense of shock and dismay.

"Doubtless," Father Spencer said, "you will recall the words of our Lord when he said that 'the first shall be last and the last shall be first', well, so it was with me."

"Father," Alfredo said, "with all due respect to your current office; in 1981 you were practically a communist and definitely an atheist."

"The term 'atheism' is such a limited, pejorative description of a complex mindset," Father Spencer said. "I prefer the term 'Anonymous Christian' as more accurately indicating my former position."

"And how," Alfredo said, "would you describe your position now?"

"Well," Father Spencer said, "the world has progressed and moved on. As have my views. I have dwelt amongst the indigenous peoples in Latin America, just as Jesus dwelt amongst the poor, tending to their needs against their Capitalist oppressors …"

"You don't mean to say you're still a Marxist?" Alfredo said, interrupting.

"Liberation theology has been sadly misconstrued by conservatives and traditionalists," Father Spencer said. "Unless one deals with the reality of a contemporary situation one cannot appreciate the necessary remedies. The preferential option for the poor is now mainstream."

Alfredo didn't want to hear any more of his modernist theology. He was no longer a school pupil, and Spencer had no power over his education. Nevertheless, it was hard to shake off the impression he was back in the classroom.

"About Father Laker … " Alfredo said.

"Long gone from what I understand," Father Spencer murmured, his reply both regretful and firm. "Sent abroad by the Holy See I think. Most likely dead by now. That funny little half-schismatic chapel of his burnt down late in 1981. Probably blamed the Freemasons for the fire too."

"Goodbye Father," Alfredo said.

Ж

After Alfredo had left the church, Father Spencer still sat there, trying to compose himself. He was badly shaken by the encounter.

Although he did not believe in the supernatural – except as a metaphor – to see that boy's piercing gaze once more, to hear again the same reactionary tripe after thirty odd years had passed, both issuing from the physical form of a forty-eight year old man! Well, it was almost like a "true" case of demonic possession.

Or perhaps a spectre personally haunting him.

Anyway, some horrible and fantastical thing from the Middle Ages.

He wondered what would happen hereafter between them, dreading the likely difficulties entailed in tending to this errant, wilful sheep amongst his parish flock.

Perhaps, Father Spencer thought, Alfredo would soon drift away to the S.S.P.X. faction who operated out of a chapel not far from the Holloway Road.

The thought was consoling. It would be Alfredo's own free will after all.

Father Spencer got up and went off to listen to the podcast of an interesting programme on the B.B.C. about the excellent new Labour leader's unexpected and overwhelming internal election success. He himself had very recently re-joined the party after many years away, in order to specifically vote in the ballot.

Ж

It was seven in the evening, when Alfredo finally reached home. He had made a diversion to the local supermarket in order to pick up food supplies and had some difficulty with the automatic check-out tills. He had kept trying to manually enter in the price of the items he wanted to purchase on the screen as the queue forming behind him shuffled their feet and tutted offensively. Eventually a member of staff came over, a gigantic black woman who was extremely helpful and patient. She showed him the secret of the barcodes and helped him laser-scan them. Alfredo realised that the impression was forming around him amongst the waiting customers that he was a mental defective rather than simply ignorant about how to pay for the goods. Presumably they had first thought he was an eccentric millionaire whose servants usually did all his shopping for him.

Later, once he had eaten his meal of oven Spaghetti Bolognese and sea-salt crisps, washed down with four glasses of lemonade, he became interested in an object he discovered in the ground floor back room. It was a black plastic-coated device about the size, weight and thickness of a coffee-table book. The thing was plugged into the mains but to what end Alfredo could not at first discover. After turning it over and examining it further he found that it opened up. The lid contained a screen and a typewriter-style Qwerty keyboard. It was obviously some sort of computer his aunt had acquired. He pressed several buttons and finally located the one that turned the machine on.

The screen lit up and he saw upon the display something like the series of icons he'd previously seen on Dorian Marsh's handheld device. However, pushing the screen with his fingers didn't seem to work and neither did pushing buttons on the keyboard one at a time. The thing appeared to him to be defective and he turned it off again.

For the rest of the evening he puffed away on his electronic cigarette-pipe and buried himself in his books. Finally sleepy, He climbed into bed long after midnight, but not before remembering to say his daily rosary (a novena for the soul of the heretic priest of St. Jerome's, and one for the souls of the Faithful Departed.)

Alfredo was troubled in the night by a recurring dream of a speeding car bearing down on him and driven by a man with no face. He awoke on a couple of occasions and called out for his aunt in a confused state of mind.

Ж

The following day he was awoken by a visit from Doctor Isaac Huntley who had been ringing the front door bell for ten minutes before Alfredo heard it, woke from his slumber, rolled out of bed, threw on the same old clothes and went below to see who it was.

He was still yawning as he pulled open the door.

Huntley looked him up and down with an air of amused self-contentment. He was carrying a couple of full shopping bags.

"You might need these," he said, sniffing. "In fact – quite obviously – I see that you do. I think I've got your size right. Same as mine."

The bags contained freshly laundered clothing.

"Some old togs I don't need," the doctor said, wandering in. "Very clean. My wife Susan was going to throw them out. How have you been getting on?"

They went into the parlour and Huntley tossed the bags onto the chesterfield.

"Perfectly well, thank you," Alfredo said.

"You realise it would be best if you were to consider seeing a counsellor. Emotional trauma is bound to surface."

"I won't do it. The decision is mine to make. Psychiatry is a lot of nonsense. It creates its own terminology for mental afflictions and then proceeds to claim to minister to them. It can't be valid."

"It's only to share your feelings after the accident and come to terms with them. Nothing else."

"I won't do it. I don't need or want it."

There was a pause.

"You're taking the paraoxitridene as prescribed?"

"Yes."

"Any symptoms – like headaches, memory loss?"

"No, not really."

"Not even from all the beer? I can still smell it on your clothes."

Huntley's actual tone was soft, without a hint of being judgmental, but the remark stung.

Alfredo shrugged as he located his electric pipe-cigarette and tried to emit a cloud of rebellion-inspired vapour. However, the light on the front started flashing showing that the battery needed recharging. Thwarted, he shoved it back into his pocket.

Huntley didn't want to antagonise his star patient. As a matter of fact his behaviour was exactly what he might have expected from any fourteen-year old who had been given license, and the financial means, to take control entirely of their own life. What concerned him most was the psychological consequences and damage Alfredo might suffer. Punctuated alcohol consumption, in itself, wasn't likely to be contraindicative to the paraoxitridene, unless Alfredo went four or five times over the recommended daily limits. However, aside from medical considerations, if his proposed book on the case were to be a viable project it was clearly necessary to be closely involved with Alfredo and not give him cause to break off all but strict doctor/patient relations.

"Well," Huntley said, "I strongly doubt alcohol in moderation will do you any harm, especially since – um – physically, you're an adult who's been a teetotaller all his life. You'd have to really go some in order to ..."

"It's a misnomer," Alfredo said, interrupting him.

"What is?"

"ALCOHOL. No one drinks alcohol. People use the word in the same sense as they do – for example – 'water'. But no one says ' I drank a glass of alcohol'."

"Anyway ..." Huntley said, feeling the subject had drifted, but Alfredo went on:

"It's an Arabic term, for an intoxicant forbidden by the creed of Islam."

"Yes, I know that."

"Take wine for example. The sacramental dimension of it, indeed all of the various sacramental aspects of the Catholic religion, are anathema to orthodox Muslims."

"And your point is?" Huntley said, wanting to get the lecture over and done with.

"Simply that ALCOHOL is, when used inaccurately, an intrinsically pejorative term."

There was a moment's silence.

Finally, having made his rather obtuse point, Alfredo seemed to lose interest in the subject.

"Do you want a cup of tea?" he said. "I think I'm neglecting my duties as a host. My aunt would have scolded me for it."

Huntley nodded and amusedly wondered to himself, whether he might be presented with a cup full of dry tea leaves.

Ж

The rest of the visit passed off more convivially. Huntley managed to get Alfredo to agree to a full series of neurological checks at the clinic in a month, to advise him at once of any difficulties and to come and have dinner with him, his wife (and a few friends) at the end of the week in their house up in Highgate Village. He even spent an extra couple of hours showing Alfredo how to operate the laptop computer in the back room, how to connect to the internet and how to set up an email address. He could decide for himself about the rest, like Facebook.

"I think," Huntley explained, "that browsing the internet for a few hours each day will be the fastest way for you to discover the changes in the world since 1981 and get you up to speed."

Alfredo looked doubtful. His recent, albeit brief, experience of accessing the web, on the occultist Dorian Marsh's smartphone, had been that it was a waste of time and energy to bother with the online world at all. The thing seemed to him to be a kind of endless comic-book for lowbrows. Nevertheless, after a moment's thought, he typed the words "Sinclair Egremont Xavier" into a search engine and began exploring the results.

He was still working his way through them, thoroughly engrossed, when Huntley had to leave. The doctor's parting words were to the effect of how very much his wife Susan was looking forward to having Alfredo over for dinner.

Ж

Alfredo was quite impressed with a blog he had discovered by a group calling themselves "Sinclair Egremont Xavier Appreciation Society". The brief bibliography of the author, used as a margin banner, appeared relatively free of errors, though Alfredo noted one or two points of contention (they had included a 1929 pamphlet probably not written by Xavier but instead by an anonymous enemy of his, as a cutting satire). The text ran as follows:

SINCLAIR EGREMONT XAVIER (1900-1970); educ. Highgate Public School, Marlborough College, Magdalen College, Oxon. Received into Roman Catholic Church, 1928. His books include *Perfectly Tight*, 1924;

Charleston? I'll Say So!, 1926; *Lady Feelgoode and the Treasure Hunt*, 1927, *A Rather Sticky End*, 1928; *Mr. Xavier Now Says No!*, 1929; *Holy See or Modern Babel*, 1930; *Mr. Xavier's Guide to Choosing Only the Best Wines*, 1931; *Not With a Bang*, 1933; *The Violation of the Holy Church in Spain*, 1936; *The Image of the Beast*, 1937; *Mr. Xavier Calls for Order*, 1939; *And Now for A Distributist England*, 1944; *Return to Maidenhead Hall*, 1946; *Soviet England*, 1952, *Completely Ghastly (An Indictment of Hollywood, its Studios and its Delinquent Motion Pictures)*, 1953; *The End of the West Pier*, 1958; *Mr. Xavier versus the Beatniks*, 1960; *Absolutely No Need for Change: Advice to the Second Vatican Council*, 1961, *Kindly Keep Off the Grass: Drugs, Youth Culture and Neo-Gnosticism*, 1967; *My Worst Fears Confirmed: An Autobiography*, 1970.

The rest of the blog consisted of a series of entries by the Chairman of the Appreciation Society, a person signing his entries pseudonymously as "Parmenides" (presumably after the Greek, Monist philosopher of antiquity) but whose real identity was easily discoverable as someone called Ernest Quinn. Although the name was unfamiliar, the blog entries contained a number of photographs taken at small social events held by the League. These tended to be visits to places frequented by, or associated with, Xavier himself. Pubs and churches seemed to feature most heavily, though there were one or two visits to private houses wherein Xavier had once lived or stayed. Quinn had been present at almost all of the events, many of which were held in London. Seeing his face repeatedly Alfredo realised he recognised it, and eventually came to the conclusion it was the same person – though obviously now considerably older – who had been trying to sell copies of *Bulldog* outside the gates of Southwood School in 1981. Since that time, Alfredo discovered, after more online searching, Quinn had turned Catholic – Traditionalist Catholic even – and written a biography and a series of critical commentaries on Xavier. A little more searching brought up an email address and Alfredo wrote and sent his first email, pointing out the contentious nature of including *Mr. Xavier Now Says No!* in the bibliography.

CHAPTER NINE

"I DON'T want him coming here," Susan Huntley said.

"Why not? You know how important this is to me," replied Isaac Huntley. "Anyway, it's only a little dinner party. And he's one guest. Alfredo's quite interesting in his own strange way."

"I don't want to know! He's a patient of yours, Isaac!" she said. "We agreed you wouldn't bring your work home under any circumstances. It's bad enough that you *disrespect* what I do – the boutique I mean – as my little unimportant hobby, without your bringing patients home."

Isaac tried not to show any reaction on his face. Frankly, he was bored rigid by even the mention of her children's clothes shop, but did appreciate that he couldn't possibly admit to it.

"But you know I've always supported you when it

comes to your boutique, darling," he said.

"Only financially! I don't even think you LIKE the idea of children," she replied. "You don't look at my designs, you don't ask about it at all unless I bring it up!"

"I've been pre-occupied of late. I'll admit that. Definitely time I did better and showed more consideration. No question about it."

She sighed. It was the same old response. It had been bad enough when Isaac had decided to start attending all those weekend medical conferences where he was in demand as a guest speaker and where she was expected to tag along as the dutiful little house-wife. Or perhaps as the trophy-wife. In fact a combination of the two. Her father, who had been a senior consultant at the Whittington Hospital during the 1970s and early 1980s, had made her own mother ill the same way in the end. He'd died quickly of pancreatic cancer in 1984 but not before reducing his wife to total dependency on him. Much like a patient in intensive care.

"He's a staunch Catholic," Isaac said, playing his trump.

She stared at him.

Isaac himself hadn't been to Mass for years. As far as it was possible to determine his beliefs he was a secular Agnostic. He looked upon the Church as a funny anachronism, rather like a circus, with the priests as creepy clowns in dresses and which now existed mostly for the benefit of the Irish and the Polish living in England. She attended Mass most Sundays, and without fail for the days of Obligation that had been moved in England to a Sunday, and made a confession at least once a year, usually before Easter. Although she had fallen out of the habit of saying the rosary she often found herself saying the Hail Mary in moments of crisis.

"Fine," she said. "Fine. Then I'll invite Father Spencer from St. Jerome's too. Meera finds him amusing. Lovely."

Isaac blanched.

He hadn't anticipated class war. The last time he had met that dotty old lefty priest over the dinner table he'd delivered a long lecture on the bloody Sandinistas. Even the other one, the American Elvis impersonator, was more tolerable than him.

Ж

Father Spencer's mobile phone made a ringing noise and vibrated itself in a small circle on his desk. He was in the little office tucked away in St. Jerome's Retreat, at the rear of the church, and going over – as he often did whenever pastoral duties didn't occupy him – the text of his unpublished memoir of his sojourn over in

Nicaragua during 1989 when he had been a newly ordained priest.

He looked away from the print-out of the manuscript and at the display on the phone. "Mrs. Huntley" it told him. It was that rather good-looking woman who turned up regularly for his seven p.m. Sunday Mass. Probably something to do again with her donating clothes for needy children.

Father Spencer picked up the phone and pressed it to his ear.

"Father Dennis here," he said. "Hello Susan."

Best to be informal.

"Hello Father," she said. "I won't keep you long. I know how terribly busy you are. I just wanted to ask if you'd like to join me and Isaac and a few friends for dinner next week; Friday evening."

"Only if it's not fish," he said, making a joke.

There was a short pause at the other end.

"Oh, I see, yes. Ha, ha," she said, without much enthusiasm.

"Hang on while I check my diary."

He flicked through the pocket book in which he wrote down his forthcoming activities. His associate priest, not him, was conducting church business that evening.

"I'd be delighted. What time exactly?"

"Eight p.m?"

"Fine, I'll see you then, if not beforehand at Mass of course. I look forward to it."

"Bye then. Thanks Father Dennis. Lovely."

"Goodbye."

He pushed the mobile phone across the desk. Something was up. She'd never invited him up to the house before. Usually it was to do with that husband of hers, the one who wasn't Catholic. Anyway, it would doubtless be a useful diversion from the norm, since the couple were very well-off and no doubt liked to put on a good spread for guests. He'd listened to her confessions a few times and was reminded of a joke made by Bishop Fulton Sheen about hearing nuns' confessions: it was like being pelted with popcorn. His American colleague at St. Jerome's, Father Chuck, had told him that anecdote. Father Chuck hailed from Memphis and spoke with a thick southern US accent. He was far more keen on C.S. Lewis than Karl Rahner, but it hadn't prevented him getting through the rigours of the seminary. He hoped his fellow priest was busy somewhere with the devout old ladies who helped the church behind the scenes and wouldn't barge in and disturb him while he was working on his own project.

Father Spencer's attention returned to the manuscript and he carried on making notes in the margins and adding corrections. He'd been at work on this new *magnum opus* for several years and was determined it wouldn't go the way of his last one, half-written back when he'd just left university, regarding the Independent Labour Party during the 1930s. Liberation theology was no longer the bugbear it had been under Pope John Paul II or under Pope Benedict XVI. Under the more enlightened tolerance of Pope Francis, himself a Latin American of course, and due to the fact that the Sandinistas had been returned to power in 2006 and re-elected in 2011, Father Spencer's memoir on his Nicaraguan experience, was, he thought, now quite timely indeed.

Ж

Ernest Quinn was slowly working his way through his correspondence. His Twitter feed had again been hijacked with abuse from pseudonymous "followers" that he had had to block after their first couple of tweets. He doubted very much they were the work of more than three or four obsessed individuals, who operated by continually adopting new false identities in order to circumvent his blocking them for good. Their assaults came from differing motives.

The first read:

"*You are still a secret fascist-nazi: ADMIT your current*

crimes and publicly apologise to all decent kind people like me. Then shut up and die." and *"We don't need your religious claptrap. No online platform for hate speechers. YOU PRICK. P.S. Read some DAWKINS."*

The second read:

"English fogey Trad-Catholic traitor. Has Pope Francis taught you nothing about loving all humanity? Why do you hate women?" then *"Misogynist idiot. Christ died for them too. Ordination of female priests in the RC now! Go back to the 12TH Century where you belong."*

The third read:

"Return to the true path of White Power, what you have sadly abandoned for the WHORE of BABILON and his Jesuit Pedos." then *"Smash the Reds, the Wogs and the Jewboys. Kick out the Towel-heads. Keep Europa racially pure. Mosley lives and MARCHES ON/88."*

There were several more, including one from a forty-eight year old stand-up comedian, who posted under his actual name, Mickey Smart, and who did the rounds of London comedy clubs. He seemed to be most concerned with getting his career going, either on B.B.C. radio or television, by pushing up the number of his leftist followers on social media. Quinn didn't recall meeting him ever, but Smart had tweeted the following remarks:

"Retract rec of Quinn book. Met him once at a party 10 yrs ago. Didn't know he was a rwing nutter. What a git. Forgive me comrades."

and he followed it up with

"Gig tmoro at the Kings Head, Crouch End, N10. 10 quid on the door. 9 P.M. start. All welcome. Not Quinn obviously. LOL."

Quinn blocked him too, but not without a pang. He knew that by doing so he was only drawing unnecessary attention to the comedian's remarks. Social media was primarily a means of drawing attention to oneself and Quinn, who had little interest in doing so, recognised nevertheless he had to have a minimal presence as a means of promoting sales of his books – his sole source of income. He lamented the fact that he had not been born a hundred years earlier when ideas were fought over in print, at length and in detail, instead of digitally, online, where reiterated insult, and appeals to a sense of outrage and progress had the final say. He had never denied his past association with the

National Front but had long ago repudiated its philosophy of deliberately inciting racial conflict, had broken off all contact with White Power movement followers, and been received into the most multinational and ethnically diverse organisation in the history of the world counted for little with his self-professed enemies.

They would only have been satisfied if he now championed the far left, which to him was just another form of cultural totalitarianism; red fascism whose true aims of dominance and hegemony were masked by a concerned expression.

Quinn had even avoided contact with the likes of the S.S.P.X. and its wilder, fragmented offshoots, remaining firmly within the mainstream of Catholicism, his one "eccentricity" being his strong sympathy for the Latin Mass Society. The worst they could say was that he was a traditionalist, and even this was a pejorative term in certain quarters. Adopting the pseudonym "Parmenides" for some articles would, he hoped, require that his arguments and opinions be taken on their own merits, without reference to Quinn's past. And, for a time, he had noted a difference.

He certainly couldn't say he was surprised that most of the members of the Sinclair Egremont Xavier League, of which he was Chairman, were not Catholic at all, but solidly secular, liberal and agnostic, with only a few exceptions. His own blog emphasised Xavier's spiritual dimension, his love for a world of values that had almost vanished and his distrust of the type of thinking that holds October must be better than June and extended this to the passage of centuries.

He checked over his email account and his eye lit upon a name he didn't recognise, heading an email forwarded from his Sinclair Egremont Xavier blog. It was from someone called Alfredo Salgado.

Dear Mr. Quinn,

You may not recall our meeting very briefly in 1981. For reasons I will not go into my recollection of the event is likely to be much more clear than yours.

However, I am not writing in that connection although I am glad to learn you have been received into the Church in the interim. I am in fact writing about your inclusion of the pamphlet Mr. Xavier Now Says No! *in the bibliographic section of your interesting blog. I number myself amongst the devotees of this excellent writer and believe that entry to be spurious. In front of me is a copy of Horace Butler's1972 memoir of Sinclair Egremont Xavier and on page 104 he clearly indicates that* Mr. Xavier Now Says No! *was a parody poking fun at the Master's conversion to Catholicism by a follower of his sometime literary nemesis, and Oxford associate, the communist Canadian author Darren*

Blair, who by 1960 was permanently incarcerated in a lunatic asylum after sexual relations with his pet husky.

Quinn considered ignoring the missive and deleting it from his inbox. The reference to 1981 told him that it was quite possibly from one of the far-right crowd with whom he'd associated back then. However, the reference to the sender being pleased to learn about Quinn's reception into the Church was not to be overlooked. This man Salgado, whoever he was, seemed to be a member of the Household of the Faith and so Quinn rattled off a quick reply. The final question of the authenticity of *Mr. Xavier Now Says No!* had actually been settled in Quinn's own biography of the Master, which Salgado had evidently not read and which was published in 2002.

Quinn briefly outlined the known facts about the publication to Salgado; that, over the course of a two week binge on champagne and claret, the Master had locked himself indoors, knocked out the infamous text on his Underwood typewriter, taken it to the printers directly himself and paid handsomely for the production, had boxes of the pamphlet sent over to his rooms at the Albany, posted a dozen copies while still drunk, before finally disappearing into the confines of Maidenhead Hall in Yorkshire to spend Christmas with Ladies Gertrude and Penelope Montague, the notorious twin flappers and wild socialites. When *Mr. Xavier Now Says No!* was found to contain not only vicious and libellous accusations but also a series of common and gross grammatical errors, the Master disowned authorship altogether and claimed it was a satire perpetuated at his expense probably by "a former Oxford aesthete and bitter rival". It was solely as a consequence of Quinn's own examination of original research material; viz, bills from Harrods, from the printing company involved, and a previously undiscovered letter to the Master from the Montague sisters that the true situation came to light.

Ж

The morning after Quinn replied to Alfredo, Susan Huntley was in her boutique on the Archway Road having just finished going over the designs for her latest range of winter jumpers for five to six year old children. Each would be unique and knitted by hand, at considerable expense, with a picture of a different cuddly animal on the front of each. As soon as she had them back from her team of knitters she decided she would give the items pride of place in the boutique window and sell them at two hundred pounds each. Most of the trade would come via her online shop, but she decided it would be an excellent idea to offer a slight discount for those customers collecting the goods from the boutique itself, since a personal visit often led to impulse buys.

This idea was doubtless prompted by the fact that she hadn't had a single customer call into the shop all morning, although this was not unusual. It was often the case that parents waited until the afternoon, when school had finished, to bring their children into the boutique. A few days back, for example, there had been a mad rush of three customers in the afternoon, and Susan had been occupied in encouraging the parents to dress up their offspring in a variety of her designs. One of the parents had spent over four hundred pounds on two items and promised to "like" the boutique on Facebook. Susan was busily trying to establish whether this person had actually done so when her friend, Meera Gupta, walked into the boutique.

Susan was surprised to see her at this time since she now kept regular nine-to-five office hours at the production department of B.B.C. Digital Radio 8 Arts, where she commissioned literary readings for a recorded programme broadcast late at night once a week on Fridays. She had three children, all girls, aged three, five and seven, but never brought them into the shop. As far as Susan could tell (by craftily examining the labels) she got them clothed off-the-peg at M&S.

Meera was a still-glamorous, highly opinionated

Asian woman in her mid thirties. She came from an Indian Hindu background and Susan supposed that this was why whenever they had touched upon religion in conversation she tended to express the firm opinion that different religions were simply "various paths up the same mountain". She was a great favourite with Father Spencer who had expressed a long-standing – though as yet not followed through – desire to accompany her to the Hindu Temple further down the Archway Road and attend one of the ceremonies. He thought it would be in the right ecumenical spirit.

"Hello Susan darling," Meera said. "I just dropped in because I thought it more polite to tell you in person rather than texting you, that I can't make Friday."

"What a shame."

"Yes, I know. Work is so busy right now. The Head of Production is away with man-flu and I've got to fill in, so much of a drag. I'll be going over recordings at home all evening on Friday. It's such a shame not to see that funny old Father Dennis. Oh and Isaac as well of course."

"It's probably for the best. He's insisting that one of his patients be there too."

"Really? How weird. Which one?"

"I don't know him. Alfredo something or other. I'm in the dark about it."

Meera, however, knew more about it than did

Susan. Old Mr. Lindop, the solicitor, had let slip the story about Issac's patient Alfredo Salgado coming out of a coma, when she'd been in the law firm's office making a codicil to her will last week. The event was probably the most exciting and unusual turn of events the elderly man had been involved with throughout his whole legal career, since the firm usually dealt solidly in dull conveyancing and probate cases. What she had heard about this Alfredo character was fascinating, and she decided that the opportunity to actually meet him was too good to pass up. There might even be a story in it that would help her with her long-desired transfer into the news journalism side of the B.B.C. She was sick to death of dealing with nothing but vain authors and obscure modern poets. That crowd were even worse than her three brats indoors who were all so self-centred and prone to tantrum-throwing it was simply hideous even to talk to them. She couldn't think where they'd got such an attitude from, but somehow society was probably to blame.

"Oh no, Susan now you've made me feel awful. I can't let you down and leave you to face the thing alone. I'll simply have to put off that work and do it all on Saturday night instead."

"Really? Lovely!"

"I'll text my mother right away and arrange for the kids to spend Friday night with her."

"Are you sure?"

"Positive. We women need to stick together you know. Eight p.m. Friday it is!"

CHAPTER TEN

IT was four in the morning and Alfredo had been surfing the internet for a solid twenty hours, puffing away continuously on his electric cigarette-pipe and fuelled by breaks for snacks and coffee. He had been seriously deflected from his proposed return to his Scholastic studies. Following Doctor Huntley's recommendation he had plunged into the task of familiarising himself with the Twenty-First Century and had rapidly come to the conclusion it was even worse than the Twentieth Century.

The fall of the Berlin Wall and the end of Soviet Communism had not meant the end of Marxism at all, but resulted in its unacknowledged inculcation even deeper into Western culture, albeit in mutated form. With the N.A.T.O. vs Warsaw Pact threat of mutually assured destruction gone, communist states themselves were no longer regarded as a definite military enemy (except for North Korea, the last remnant of a Stalinist "cult of personality"). The ideologues who had once supported communism now transferred their political campaign from the economic into the cultural arena. As far as Alfredo could see even the new leader of the Labour Party (apparently its most leftist leader since Foot) was not calling for the total abolition of private enterprise in favour of proletarian ownership of all means of production – at least, not yet.

Perhaps the most startling evidence of this, in Alfredo's eyes, was the huge popularity of Euro and National Lotteries, which could turn someone from a pauper into a multi-millionaire overnight, week in week out, and to which people looked as their only salvation. It seemed to have replaced entirely the old Football Pools, even though the particular sport behind it now appeared to have achieved a media prominence and mass fascination he found repulsive to contemplate.

People on the left had accepted wholly the assumption that great personal wealth (when held, for example, by celebrities or entertainers, rather than by bankers or other businessmen, despite both doing so via the same evil of Capitalism) was excusable. What was important was the individual's adherence to a behavioural code presented – in its most propagandistic form – as simply being "progressive". The code advanced its boundaries decade through decade, without the populace much noticing save for each new development being itself a sign of "progress". The basic mode of operation appeared to be centred around values being repositioned from moral bases into ones concerned solely with cultural equality. This was the creed of the proglodytes.

If propositions are framed in terms of an imperative "Equal rights for all" then it was entirely possible to see how only an unexamined agenda could operate under that cover. "Equal rights for all" was a logically inconsistent proposition. It would also entail equal rights (e.g. free expression for all) for those wishing to abolish equal rights (e.g. to abolish free expression). In fact, what it resulted in was the old Orwellian sense that "some are more equal than others."

Not, of course, thought Alfredo, that the process hadn't been going on in the West decades before the 1980s. It first fully gained command of the cultural field twenty years earlier. But the 1960s wasn't the start of anything revolutionary, it was a dead-end that has lasted (thus far) for fifty years. We are still living, culturally, in the 1960s. The Anti-Establishment is now the Neo-Establishment, who are so locked into the idea of permanent rebellion they can't bring themselves to see, let alone, admit, the truth.

During the hours that Alfredo had spent online,

the most astonishing development he had noted was the rise of Islam in the West and the convoluted nature of the Neo-Establishment's relationship with it.

He began making notes, scrawling out his impressions and ideas in one of the blank exercise books dating from 1981. On the front of it he wrote Purgatory Is the 21st Century.

Ж

"One of the reasons militant Islam has taken such hold in Europe is because of the increasing spiritual vacuum left by the long legacy of the (so-called) Enlightenment. I find it highly ironic that the secularist Neo-Establishment of the E.U. thought it a grand idea to offset the demographic decline in the birthrate of the continent's indigenous populace by importing millions of Muslims from around the world to bolster the workforce of the European economy.

With radical Leftist ideas having been the driving force behind revolutionary radical movements in the Middle East for decades, I imagine our political masters thought all the Muslims would eventually assimilate within a generation or so, wholly embrace the void of Western secularism, throw over their deeply ingrained tradition and become good little consumerists and techno-zombies – just like the rest of the European populace who have been subjected to decades of state-sanctioned ideological secular schooling, the metropolitan mass-media, and the peer-pressure of group-think. The acceptable boundaries had been so far pushed back that the laughable "reactionary" forces, the likes of Fox News, *The Daily Mail*, and U.K.I.P. were taken seriously as a real contemporary opposition and threat, when, in fact, even they were extolling current ideas and values that would have seemed highly "progressive" to leftist-liberal circles a few decades ago. The ideological juggernaut of secularism has rolled over all obstacles.

"But it's not worked out quite as our political and cultural masters planned with Islam, and for this reason: Islam is absolutely impervious to the philosophical assault of Enlightenment values in a way that Christianity was not. Why is this? Simply because Enlightenment values specifically developed out of our own European Christian heritage, particularly via Protestantism and Anti-Clericalism. Centuries removed from its first throes of life in the French Revolution and the Scottish non-conformist tendencies, the Enlightenment project can be seen exactly by Muslim scholars for what it actually is; a phased programme moving from Deism via watery Voltairean Theism to the end-goal of Materialism, Atheism and the elimination of revelation, authority and eternal law from serious consideration for all time.

"Mosques, many of them radicalised, have been and are being erected in Europe at a rate that must give even ardent secularists pause for thought. Complete separation of church and state is a Western fetish. The Prophet Muhammed was not only a visionary, he was also a soldier and a political leader. I suspect we are eventually going to see conversion rates from secular unbelief to Islam jump dramatically amongst the native populations of Europe. The weak tend to worship the strong. The people of any country, once it has turned Islamic, never abandon that faith. They know, and accept, that the penalty of apostasy from Islam in an Islamic State is death. Islam, once established, will simply not allow any alternative. It may tolerate a small number of non-Muslims in its midst, but they will have no significant political power whatsoever. Moreover, Islam – historically – advanced not via conversions but either by force of arms or by force of numbers.

"Europe is practically finished as a Christian continent. We, and no-one else, betrayed our own cultural and religious heritage. The worldly forces that are arraigned against it have become all-powerful, all-pervasive and are in triumph. Perhaps the greatest trick the current secularist power has pulled is to claim it is fighting some kind of rebellion against the oppressive forces of the Old Establishment when the secularist power is itself now the ruling Neo-Establishment.

"The response will be typical. It is to rapidly change the subject and shift the argument along the lines of "let's address the real issue: you are a traditionalist Catholic. You desire the restoration of the Middle Ages. If you had your way Christianity would return to a position of power and privilege. Jews and so-called heretics burnt alive in the Spanish Inquisition. Women too, across Christendom, tortured and killed as witches. Your damn Pope would be ultramontane and omnipotent. All the evils of the Church would come crawling back centuries after we secularists had driven them out. *So do not presume to preach to us about the 'sanctity' of human life.*"

"Why are these examples so powerful? Do they not stand out vividly precisely because they represent glaring deviations from a universal moral standard within Christendom that contained the worst excesses of which human beings are capable?

"And the truth of the matter is simply this: centuries of Catholic civilisation, even with all its worst features, cannot be compared, in scale and numbers, with the alternate nightmare of just one secularist century, the twentieth, with its procession of Nazi concentration camps, U.S. atomic attacks on Hiroshima and Nagasaki, Soviet Gulags and state-directed famines, European abortion clinics, the Chinese cultural revolution, and the Cambodian genocide, a list by no means exhaustive. But what do all these atrocities have in common? One very simple underlying thing, the creed that is at the heart of secularist modernity: human beings are biological cogs in an economic machine and 'some are more equal than others'.

"If morality is framed solely in terms of class, national identity or biology then there are no limits to the assault we feel we can wreak upon "the enemy". And the twentieth century demonstrates this beyond any doubt.

"Perhaps the greatest success of modernity is that it has achieved something previously believed impossible. It has turned an assumptive agenda into an all-pervasive ideology that *is designed not to be recognised by the vast majority of its own adherents but is nevertheless drilled into them by means of continuous – and often subliminal – propaganda.* It is like a new attempt at a Soviet Union wherein one system is taught and practised but is never actually acknowledged as being the only acceptable ideology. Indeed, part of its agenda is to give the impression that it allows diversity of thought. However, its very essence is that it must limit the opportunity of expression for any radical divergence from its own ideological range to an absolute minimum. This it does not through the clumsy, obvious and brutal system of rubber truncheons and secret police, but through having achieved such a high level of self-policing within those subjected to its propaganda that *all divergent analyses fall on deaf ears and are marginalised as a consequence of mass-indoctrinating the principle of contempt prior to examination.*

"It may be argued that these same objections can be levelled at monotheism. Secularists often contend that religion only persists because it is "indoctrinated" into children. However, there are several clear historical cases wherein attempts to stamp out religion, through prohibiting it being taught in schools, have occurred. To take the best known example, in the Soviet Union, for almost seven decades, a whole lifetime, communism not only forbade by law and punishment the teaching of Christianity to children, the state also actively indoctrinated children against it with doctrinaire Marxist atheism. However, Christianity survived underground, and immediately saw a resurgence at the end of the Soviet Empire.

"The ideology of contemporaneity has successfully inculcated an attitude of mind in the mass of its indoctrinated supporters wherein totalitarianism possesses a 'kind' face. It is the vindication of the truth about brainwashing. Brainwashing does not succeed unless the brainwashed are made to absolutely believe that they have not been duped at all but are actually in full possession of the truth. Hence it is not necessary to define towards what end "progress" is advancing, or within which limits it may operate, only that "progress" cannot be questioned.

"This western Leftist ideology consists of a series of interlinked political thought ranging from the likes of Identity Politics, Isaiah Berlin's 'Negative Freedom', Neo-Liberalism and the Frankfurt School. These theories rise and fall, each leaving a trace in the culture as it is either subsumed, revised or synthesised. Each has its own degree of prominence and emphasis, but all contribute to the overarching tapestry of ideological contemporaneity. The objection may be raised that this scarcely sounds anything like a coherent ideology, since not only are the various currents of thought mentioned opposed to one another in certain important features but that they are too diffuse, taken overall, to constitute anything other than facets of modern thought itself.

"And the crux of the matter is this: Contemporaneity cannot be anything other than atomised since it actually aims at the elimination of an Absolute. By doing away with an objective normative standard by which truth and morality can be determined, it overcomes its greatest foe. Any 'truth' can be promoted within the confines of its own predicates on the basis of unexamined assumptions. If someone disagrees, he is regarded as not doing so honestly, not having examined the other side's position, and because that person is 'of the enemy', whether that enemy be one of class, race or gender.

"Let us return to the question of the place of the Catholic Church in all this.

"The struggle of traditionalist Catholicism is not remotely a question of re-establishing the Middle Ages in Europe and the Papal ultramontanism of the late Nineteenth Century. Such a thing is almost impossible to achieve. The overwhelming modernist forces arraigned against it are so embedded in power (both within and without the Church) that only a complete collapse of Western civilisation, with all the misery that would result from it, could bring about such a restoration. It is also utterly undesirable since it would entail, in contemporary socio-cultural conditions, a degree of violent coercion abhorrent to the essence of the Christian Faith itself and more akin to Bolshevism. Rather it is a case of the Church's very survival in the face of mounting persecution. Across the globe Christians are once again being vilified and put to death. However, the Church, being of supernatural foundation, cannot be destroyed. The triumph of Christianity is, in the end, of a spiritual and sacramental nature. And if all the churches in Europe empty out and are reduced to rubble or a handful of museums scattered across the world, it makes no difference to the truth of the Gospel message. In its earliest days the followers of Christ sought refuge in the catacombs and if again, in the last days, we must once more return to the catacombs, still the Faith will endure. Our way is not submission to the Prince of this World but instead to defy him and his works.

"Recall the words of Pius XII: "I go this way fully conscious of my weakness, believing in Him who uses the weak to put the strong to shame. What I was, is nothing; what I am is little; but what I shall become is eternal."

Ж

Alfredo put down his pen, stretching the cramped muscles in his hand. His brain had been working at a fantastic rate to assimilate all the information he'd been starved of during the period of his fugue-state or coma. It was like an uncontrollable hunger.

The radio in the background was reporting on a series of mass shootings in Paris by Islamist terrorists who were firing indiscriminately at human targets. Alfredo listened for a while, appalled, and then turned it off. As soon as the expressions of regret over the killings were finished, concerns were immediately raised about the 'real' danger of what a commentator described as "a Europe-wide 'Nazi' backlash" and she brought up some lone-wolf murderer called Anders Breivik to justify her provocative remarks so soon after the atrocity.

He staggered upstairs, said his evening prayers (Psalm 129, *De Profoundis*), mourned for the loss of life and crawled into bed, utterly mentally exhausted. That night, he did not dream.

Ж

Alfredo attended Mass the following day at St. Jerome's. It was not officiated by Father Spencer but by another priest, an American with a very thick deep-South accent and whom Alfredo did not know. Since it was an evening, weekday Mass attendance was sparse, with only a few worshippers dotted here and there across the vast expanse of wooden pews. There was not a mantilla in sight. No censer billowed clouds of mystic incense to spiritually cleanse the altar. The priest stood alone and faced the congregation, his back to the altar and to the Holy of Holies.

Alfredo tried to keep his attention fixed on the flickering red light of the tabernacle, concentrating his thoughts on prayer. He had, of course, anticipated that it would be a *Novus Ordo* liturgy, but the reality was not something he had previously experienced and the strangeness of it was almost unbearable. His aunt had been insistent on their attending the (so-called) Extraordinary Form of the Mass, in Latin, and, prior to becoming regular communicants at the Chapel of Pope St. Zosimus, their Mass-going had been a peripatetic affair. They had attended ceremonies at, amongst others, St. James in Spanish Place, the Brompton Oratory and St. Etheldreda's in Ely Place, travelling all across London in search of an ancient form of worship now as rare as it had been for the loyal Catholic recusants who had been martyred under the reign of Queen Elizabeth I.

As he sat, knelt and prayed in the church Alfredo tried to follow the Mass in his heavy, gilt-edged and bible-black 1957 Missal from the Pontificate of Pope Pius XII, glancing at the Latin margins, but so much of the liturgy had been altered he was forced to pick up one of the wholly English vernacular modern Daily Mass paperbacks littering the place in order to make sure his ears weren't deceiving him. The dull translations into English that were being spoken by the priest and the loud responses from the people around him wouldn't have been out of place in a Methodist chapel. He put the book back down.

Someone, a business man in an expensive suit, lounging in the next pew, actually began to slouch. On the far left side of the aisle a bored youth in a hooded jogging top, sat next to his mother, was surreptitiously texting away on his smartphone. At the back a half-deaf elderly woman was loudly conversing with her companion. Doubtless, as some theological Modernists might contend, they were still paying homage to Christ in their own way. Only one man, in his sixties, seemed wholly absorbed in the liturgy, the responses and the act of worship.

He was dressed shabbily, in a shapeless grey nylon jacket and baggy trousers. His head was bald, his eye-glasses held together with gaffer tape. Half his face was obscured by a white beard. He uttered the responses in an Irish accent, clearly and reverently, without raising his voice. It was obvious that his whole attention was focused on the ritual and on fulfilling his own part in the Mass to the utmost of his ability.

However, Alfredo rebuked himself for his distraction and stared fixedly at the altar and the priest, forcing himself not to pay attention to those around him, and trying to recall, as his aunt had repeatedly instructed him, that the Holy Mass is a prayer in itself.

At one point, in his ecumenical homily, the American priest droned on about the attacks in France the previous night, and about all men and women of faith having far more in common than that which divided them.

During the moment when the worshippers offered one another a sign of peace, Alfredo, confused by the novelty, dropped to his knees, closed his eyes and appeared to ignore those around him, though he was actually deep in silent prayer.

At the communion, Alfredo also caused something of a minor delay in the short, fast-moving queue by kneeling in front of the priest as he received the blessed host on his tongue, being the only person to do so.

And when the Mass was ended he tried to exit before the priest could get to the porch outside ahead of him, but wasn't quite quick enough since the American half-ran down the aisle to overtake him.

Ж

Outside the priest extended his hand and Alfredo glanced at it with apparent disinterest, but he was actually still meditating over his unworthiness to receive the sacraments, and not really aware of the gesture until it was withdrawn after a pause.

"Ah reckon you must be Alfredo," he said. "Father Spencer done told me all about yew."

A few of the parishioners drifted out, and hung around outside, watching – slightly agog – at the scene.

"That's so, Father," he said.

"Tradishunalist, huh?"

"I'm afraid this is the first Catholic church I've been inside without an altar rail at which to kneel when the blessed sacrament is offered to the Faithful."

"Never unnerstood it. Lot of folks back home like yew. Don't like renewal. Hidebound. But we're all Gawd's childrun, Ah reckon. If yew genewflect tew tha Host why not tew tha peeple also?"

"By 'renewal' I would contend that you actually mean theological Modernism."

"Yew obviously familiar with liturjekal history," said the priest. "So doubtless yew aware that tha New Testament was 'riginally written colloquial-like, mighty easy to understand, in Greek an' not in Latin. Tha furm of the Mass in old times, right about tha age of tha

Apostles an' all, was right simple, as it is naw, an' made fur tha peeple to unnerstan'. Not like wid tha Tridentine."

Alfredo frowned.

"It is due to respect for your office though not for your argument," Alfredo said, "that I am forced to remind you that Thomas Cranmer, sworn enemy of our Church and its Holy Mass, would have agreed with you in every particular of your argument in favour of the local vernacular."

Some of the parishioners began mumbling amongst themselves.

"S.S.P.X. probably."

"Rude."

"No sign of peace."

"Show some respect."

And Alfredo then rapidly departed, without another word. The puzzled, concerned, and grim gazes of the small crowd and the priest remained.

Meanwhile, inside the church, still meditating on the blessed sacrament he had received, oblivious to all else, the old man in the grey nylon jacket knelt down on the wooden frame in front of a large crucifix mounted on a side wall and began to say, in post-communion prayer:

"Behold, O kind and most sweet Jesus, etc."

CHAPTER ELEVEN

FATHER Spencer was quietly going over the manuscript of his *magnum opus* about liberation theology in Central America when the American priest, Father 'Chuck' Driscoll, unceremoniously barged into the office. He shut off the soothing background noise of sitar music emanating from the digital radio, re-tuned it to a loud rock station, and then slumped noisily into an armchair facing the desk where Father Spencer was working. The latter tried not to allow his features to display any sign of the immense displeasure he felt at being interrupted in this way, and at the inconsideration the American priest displayed in disturbing what little free time he had to himself in the evenings.

"Done gone and met that weird fellah yew mentioned, tha – erm – brain-damaged one," Father Chuck said.

"You mean Alfredo Salgado?" he replied absently, gazing down at the papers spread out before him, in the hope the American might take the hint and clear off.

"Damn right. Made a ruckus of mah Mass. Waddaya say to it?"

"He was like that when he was a pupil in my classes, back at Southwood School, still, there's not much that can be done about it. This is a church and he can hardly be expelled for bad behaviour."

"Den, I ain't talking at all about excumunikatin' him – as yew well know. Hell, that's a Bishop's bisnis, ain't no call fur that," Father Chuck said.

Father Spencer winced at the abbreviation of his Christian name. The text of the pages in front of him on the desk began to wander from his thoughts as the American droned on, with his accent like some Elvis Presley impersonator.

"No, c'mon Den, what Ah'm saying is that mah congreegayshun was mighty upset by it. An' I got me an obligation to that stray sheep also."

"Look, I wouldn't worry about it."

Defeated by the distraction, Father Spencer shuffled the pages before him into a neat orderly pile and gazed at Father Chuck, giving him his full attention.

"I expect," Father Spencer went on, "that his main complaint is about the Mass not being in Latin. Am I right?"

"Damn right. Ah reckon he wuz thinkin' that way fur sure. Entitled to his view ah reckon, but it's a shame.

"Well, there you are. Now he knows we don't go in for all that reactionary stuff, he won't be back. He'll go off in search of one of those regressive Indult services or wind up at the S.S.P.X. chapel near Holloway Road. Problem solved. That's what he's used to doing anyway."

"Ah dunt wunt it on mah conshunce if he joins up wit' tha S.S.P.X. folks. They got too much of tha lettah of tha law and not enuff of tha spirit. This is his Parish Church also. It don't sit right wit' me, endin' like that."

"Don't you concern yourself. They've already had their own splinter groups break off. They're falling apart. Long-term, the Pope has it all in hand. I read recently that he's going to allow them to validly hear confession and give absolution for a whole year. Eventually, the bulk of them will end up back in the fold. Without being able to appoint any new bishops, mind, except under the Vatican II up-to-date rites of consecration. That way the thing will either be dead in half a century or else as irrelevant and marginalised as the Sedevacantists."

Father Chuck was strangely silent and turning the whole matter over in his mind, much like chewing a piece of fresh gum.

Father Spencer himself couldn't help but suddenly think back to his days before the priesthood and recall all the multitudinous inter-warring parties of the far-Left, each of which had claimed to be the sole possessors of true Marxist principles.

Ж

At home, in the house on Causton Road, while Fathers Spencer and Driscoll were discussing him, Alfredo was looking at himself in a bathroom mirror and trimming his beard over the wash basin. He worked with a pair of old nail scissors, pulling at little clumps of the follicles between finger and thumb, and then cutting them.

When he was finished he washed away the debris in the sink and went downstairs into the rear parlour in order to check his email correspondence. His inbox contained only one new item; a reply from Ernest Quinn in answer to his query about *Mr. Xavier Now Says No!*

Alfredo looked it over quickly and then re-read it.

There was a dull throb in the back of his head as he realised that Quinn knew rather more than he did about the authorship of the book and the case for its having been genuinely written by Sinclair Egremont Xavier. Alfredo had been refuted, albeit in a friendly fashion. He felt extremely put out at having been led into error by the Horace Butler memoir of 1972. Locating the volume on his shelves, he found page 104 wherein the false assertion of authorship by Darren Blair (or some follower of his) had been reproduced, and scrawled a disclaimer in capital letters in the margin alongside the offending passage. Then he returned to the laptop computer and rattled off a reply to Quinn.

Dear Mr. Quinn

I am obliged to you for your informative reply to my query about the inclusion of Mr. Xavier Now Says No! in the bibliography reproduced on your internet blog. Needless to say, I have not had the benefit of examining your own biography of the great Sinclair Egremont Xavier published in 2002, having been myself in a coma for a few decades and thus unable to keep up with all the developments in this field of literary study. I am naturally very keen to peruse your biography for myself. I would prefer a signed copy for my book collection of Xavierana, which item I would be glad to purchase from you directly, if available. I should, of course, be prepared to pay extra for the signature. I, too, am a staunch traditionalist Catholic and cannot abide the Age of the Modern Man which the Master so detested. I am glad that, after your association with Nationalism in your youth, you have come to see that the path of struggle is inwardly spiritual, not outwardly political.

Alfredo glanced over the missive for errors, clicked on send and then closed the lid of the computer.

He leant back in the canvas easy-chair, his mind going over the recent scene with the American priest on the porch outside St. Jerome's. It was troubling to his conscience. He should at least have offered his own hand for the priest to shake after the misunderstanding and regretted not doing so. Was it, in fact, a sin of omission on his part?

Finally he knelt down, crossed himself, fumbled in his pocket, and took out his rosary, running the beads through his fingers, mouthing the litany of prayers and meditating on the Glorious Mysteries.

Ж

"Well, there certainly could be a story in it Meera," Freddie Sutton said. "But I can't promise anything."

There was trouble brewing. Sutton could sense it.

The two of them were seated in Sutton's office at the production department of B.B.C. Radio 7 Domestic

News Digital. It was one of the few departments left in central London after the transfer of most operations up to Salford in Manchester.

"Budgets are tight across the corporation," he went on. "Our funding's already been slashed by a third over the last quarter."

"There IS a story in it all right. I'm convinced of it," she said. "It's got a great angle. Salgado is a boy from 1981 dropped into 2015, with the open mind of a fourteen year old and the brain and body of a forty-eight year old. How is that NOT a story? No one else has covered it because no one else has found out about it yet."

"There's the subject's privacy to consider," Sutton replied. "I'm not sure what you're proposing to do is ethical. It's undercover journalism really."

For months now Sutton had been aware that Meera Gupta was agitating for a transfer from radio drama into news journalism. His small staff of journalists were themselves struggling to justify their positions due to considerable overlap with other B.B.C. news journalism platforms. Adding Meera Gupta to the staff would simply add to the criticisms coming his way from management higher up in the corporation.

"You know as well as I do that R7DND is woefully under-represented in terms of diversity. Are you sure that you're considering my pitch on its own merits?"

Meera said.

Sutton shifted in his chair. He should have brought someone else into the interview as an independent witness. He could see where this was heading.

"Out of your staff of six you have just one Afro-Caribbean. All the rest are white Oxbridge men like you. I don't think you are capable of a fair appraisal. If one of your 'chums' had come to you with my pitch you'd have jumped at the opportunity. You're a drag on progress."

"I'm not sure that's entirely fair …"

"And you're part of the old Establishment. Well, buster, for your information the world is changing. I didn't want to have to bring it up but you leave me no choice. You have to face up to the reality."

She paused, cleared her throat and went on.

"I believe you're a misogynist. Possibly even a Neo-Masculinist. And I'm not going to keep quiet about it. No way."

Sutton was caught in a trap. On one level he found himself agreeing with her. What could he know of the obstacles his kind – institutionally-conditioned and privileged men – unconsciously put in the way of aspiring women? He, with his public school background, his social life revolving exclusively in upper-class circles, his quiet cottage in a secluded Kent hamlet, living comfortably with a twenty-two year old blond Adonis who himself worked part-time in Conservative Party H.Q.?

If she made her accusations in a formal complaint, management would have the perfect excuse to initiate an enquiry and then use it as a pretext for "restructuring" (i.e. "downsizing") his already tiny department.

It was being made very clear by the Trust to everyone at the B.B.C. that the new policy of positive discrimination towards women was top priority. Their representation was absolutely crucial in displaying the corporation's progressive commitment to diversity. All across the airwaves, and in all departments, the changes were dramatic. Even the last bastion – sports coverage featuring male teams – had been made to accept female commentators and pundits as part of an unofficial quota system as old male duffers shuffled off into retirement. The average football or cricket fan who couldn't care less about politics was going to ethically benefit from the internal cultural revolution, whether he liked it or not. And if he didn't like it, there would soon be nowhere else for him to go anyway. The independent commercial broadcasters would all follow in the wake of the B.B.C. eventually. 'Auntie' was the voice of the nation; she always knew best. She waved a flag of political neutrality even as she declared that only her version of tolerance would be tolerated. There might be a handful of beneficiaries who privately wondered whether they, as women, were being patronised by this unofficial quota system, and who looked back guiltily to those previous women who had risen solely due to their own outstanding ability, but any who actually came out and said so would be damned as anti-feminist traitors to the cause. It simply wasn't, thought Sutton, worth the hassle.

However, he made one last show of token resistance.

"Don't you rather think this is blackmail?"

"Blackmail," Meera replied, "is an inherently racist word coming from the likes of you. It's a term agents of the hegemonic power resort to in order to try and discredit radical opposition in action."

"Did you make up that definition yourself? It's quite convoluted."

"No, I can't say I did. I saw a sister quote it on a *Searchlight* twitter feed and memorised it for future use."

He soon caved in completely to all her demands.

Ж

Coincidentally, the day following Meera Gupta's interview with Freddie Sutton, Alfredo decided to throw out his radio.

At first he had found the device useful when he rested from studying his books of Scholasticism. But after a week he realised he was being bombarded with propaganda wherein the opinions and programming being broadcast were strictly confined inside contemporary ideological boundaries. Even so-called historical programmes "read history backwards" and re-interpreted situations from a modern perspective, rather than the context of their own times. An hour of two of listening to the radio every day would not suffice, generally, for a person to recognise that any such narrow agenda existed. For all a casual listener knew, the same propaganda was not repeated hour after hour, day in, day out. But across all the stations the same features of a universal editorial policy were repeated over and over again. Even those frequent representatives from minority communities, put on air supposedly to represent diverse viewpoints, peddled the same Neo-Establishment mantras.

Alfredo was acutely conscious of it even when he tried to resort to listening only to classical music stations, but even that was all too often punctuated with the same discussions and the same news bulletins, with the exact same priorities, as with the other stations. He dreaded to think what the television channels were like, but had no way of confirming his fears, since there was no set in the house. He recalled sitting and watching the dire Open University afternoon broadcasts on the television whenever he had been ill and off school.

And Doctor Huntley's suggestion for familiarising himself with current events via the internet had proved no less unbearable. Alfredo had allowed himself to be slowly drawn into an online world of commercial advertising and the ill-informed rhetoric or mindless propaganda of both left and right wilfully seeking grievances. Beneath the whole edifice there lurked a hellish underworld of video pornography that Alfredo had stumbled across by accident after clicking on an apparently innocuous link. Nothing demonstrated more clearly the atomised nature of contemporaneity than that sphere of disinformation exchange.

He resolved not to have anything further to do with it except for exchanging email communications.

It was no surprise that a great swathe of day-to-day activities that had existed and operated effectively (albeit less rapidly) without the internet all had now been transferred online. The whole system provided a much more direct means of monitoring, surveillance and control of the whole population. The only "benefit" to be derived from it was either financial enrichment or success in mass attention-seeking gambits, and Alfredo had no interest in either.

He was convinced that the last few days he had spent trying to catch up with the twenty-first century had been a waste of time. Nothing had changed substantially except on a cosmetic level. His recent thoughts had been committed to his notebooks wherein he wrote the following:

"The sole "advances" since 1981 have been on a technological level and each new development in "efficiency" only served to make people more and more dependent on fetishistic gadgets that were outdated or self-obsolete within a year and had to be replaced. Cultural values had been firmly embedded in the West during the 1960s and were now enshrined in what seemed to be an approximation of a "revolution" in which the "intelligentsia" are the new vanguard. However, this vanguard knows no limits when it comes to accumulating wealth for its own adherents, since it regards itself as a kind of neo-proletariat, the old proletariat having failed to carry out its part in the historic revolutionary communist destiny as predicted by classical Marxism. The incredible part of all this was that it was signally never remarked upon by those opinion-formers in positions of power and influence who upheld the ideology, but was simply taken as self-evident. Wealth is best when in the hands of the elite vanguard. And furthermore, the vast majority of those outside the elite vanguard who were blindly promoting its tenets would have denied they were doing so, and were often making the claim in all honesty, because the ideology had become the default position.

"But, even if one recognised the agenda, there was nowhere to go where one's warnings would not fall on deaf ears, except to the far margins, where, floundering in isolated and underground hatred, lurked the tiny remnants of the extreme right with their repugnant, rightly discredited, biological race-fanaticism. If one crossed that Rubicon, one became the mirror image of all that one was resisting in the extreme left. In cultural terms, this shattered remnant of rightist-totalitarianism was insignificant, even as a protest or pressure group. It had no institutional power whatsoever. Now and again some crazed lone-wolf gunman would pick up a rifle and murder his way into the news headlines, and, each time they did so, the "intelligentsia" would point to it as indicative of the inevitable rise of a new wave of actual Nazism in Europe or the United States, a nightmare scenario that could only be prevented by direct action; by blacklisting and shaming into silence for good all those who dared to disagree with them.

"The forces of the leftist cultural hegemony need the illusory threat of a resurgent fascist totalitarianism. If there wasn't enough real fascism left in existence to form a credible opposition, and thus justify pushing forward with more urgency their own project, they would do two things: vastly exaggerate the influence of what little remained or else widen the boundaries of what constitutes "fascism". Why had Left-terrorism gradually disappeared? Why were there no more military groups akin to the Red Army Faction left in the West? The reason appeared obvious. Their ideologies now exercised power and influence within the Establishment itself.

"Even the Catholic Church had been steadily infiltrated after Vatican II. The council was the pretext for an ongoing ideological invasion of the 'hermeneutics of renewal' by fellow travellers influenced by the ideas of Antonio Gramsci and the Frankfurt School. Father Dennis Spencer was a prime example of the consequences.

Ж

Alfredo stopped writing. He wasn't sure of the extent to which he was convinced by his own thesis. He recognised that he existed intellectually outside of the socio-cultural structure he was criticising, with no vested interest in it. But if this apparently gave him an advantage over others, i.e. those within, at least when it came to recognising and challenging certain of its features, he was also aware of the dangers of slipping into conspiracy theories. The conclusions of the paranoiac, though often highly internally consistent, were dependent upon precisely not being in possession of all the facts; or, perhaps, rather, of ruthlessly filtering out or of discounting, before prior examination, those objections that do not fit the pattern of the schemata.

Alfredo certainly did not think that there was a single force directing contemporaneity. The hegemony was amorphous, not unified; atomised, not cohesive. It clutched at any new "progressive" idea as it came along, absorbing it within the correct political "narrative" so far as it undermined tradition. But he could not, for example, subscribe to such outlandish nonsense that there really existed the likes of an all-powerful, highly-organised cabal of esoteric Freemasons or Zionists acting as a single "hidden hand". He didn't see that there was any coherent third-party "direction" behind it all, as such. True, certain related ideological theories accelerated a process that was already under way long before the 1960s. But what was occurring, Alfredo thought, was the dissolution of European civilisation itself, and it was being driven from within, not from without. In seeking to arrest its own terminal decline, the culture had latched onto the type of short-term solution described in the old adage "the operation was successful but the patient died."

And the operation was the endless distraction from Eternity.

Ж

Needing fresh air and exercise, Alfredo left the house and began walking through the back streets between the Archway Road and Highgate Village. He passed up the incline of Peacock Lane, circled around Southwood Lawn Road, and then across Shepherd's Hill and down into Priory Gardens. He was annoyed that he got out of breath so easily. His fourteen year old form would have scarcely registered the rise and fall of the streets, but now he struggled with tramping uphill. The afternoon was mild with no wind, and a dull grey cloud sheet spread high overhead. It was one of those English skies that existed not to produce rain but only in order to thwart sunshine. His aunt had complained to him often about them.

When Alfredo reached the top of the steep, narrow path that ran alongside Highgate Underground Station, he was spotted by Dorian Marsh, who was smoking a roll-up cigarette and leaning against the metal handrail at the summit. As usual, he carried an orange plastic bag filled with his pamphlets and other junk. He seemed to have been waiting for Alfredo to arrive.

"Do what thou wilt shall be the whole of the law.

Oh, hullo Alfredo," Marsh said, grinning and displaying unselfconsciously the gap in his bottom front teeth. "Saw you heading in this direction, while I jumped the fence down there and was looking over the old abandoned railway station for purposes of research."

The derelict remains of the old above-ground station, which had formed part of the Northern Heights railway, were strictly off-limits to the public, Alfredo would have thought. Although the platforms and a few structures remained, the tracks had been pulled up long ago and weeds, brambles and other vegetation had flourished. The idea of this old man "jumping the fence" appeared unlikely. It was several feet high and the grounds were probably monitored by functionaries watching on those security cameras that were now almost omnipresent. There were tunnels leading into the old station grounds, which, Alfredo knew, were situated on the Parkland Walk off Northwood Road, but the gates were locked shut at both ends.

"Anyway, this is good fortune. Bumping into you I mean," Dorian said.

Alfredo stared and said nothing. He was thinking over their last encounter.

"Not slipping back into a waking coma are you, I hope? Let's go into the Woodman and have a drink," he said. "I want to tell you more about the Magisteriarti. Help with your education and that."

It was only just past three in the afternoon. Alfredo was not convinced that he wished to drink at that hour, since he was concerned that he would not see a reason to stop once he started, and the rest of the day would then be wasted. However, Marsh's spontaneous mention of his pet conspiracy theory seemed to follow on remarkably from the ideas Alfredo had been jotting down in his notebooks. Perhaps it was providentially ordained that he should encounter Marsh again at exactly this juncture. It might be intriguing to debate his own conclusion that the essence of modernity was a confused amorphous mess rather than its being directed by a single guiding movement as Marsh claimed.

A few minutes later they were settled at a table at the back of the Woodman pub with drinks bought by Alfredo.

"Good health! I suppose you'll have read my publications by now," Dorian said, after swallowing a mouthful of his double Jamesons. "Just the basics are all explained in there though. Of course the real top-end secrets are only known to higher degree initiates – *and* myself."

Since Alfredo had scarcely looked at the pamphlets he shook his head.

"You disappoint me, my old son," Marsh said. "In a world gone mad you need to follow the true path of

229

sanity."

"When you talk about 'higher degree initiates'," Alfredo said, "do you mean something connected with Grand Orient Freemasonry? I should point out that I am not really interested in hearing a lot of speculation connecting them with the Bilderberg Group and with global finance capitalism. Nor do I think it logically sustainable to – as it were – join up all the 'so-called dots' and claim the world is run by an international Zionist conspiracy."

Marsh raised his eyebrows. He forced a grin but inwardly he began setting up his psychic self-defences. Visualising a wall of swirling symbols between them, modelled on the ancient mandalas of the mystic Far East, he steeled himself for what he thought was an encounter with what might well be an envoy of the Magisteriarti itself. He had battled for decades against its growing influence but only now, it seemed, when his powers were at their occult height, had they finally sent one of their own – in person rather than by email or text – to parley with him. The Magisteriarti must have taken over Alfredo's brain while he was in that waking coma state.

Well, their envoy would soon realise he was dealing with a true Ipsissimus and not some novice who'd only just mastered the VIII degree of the OTO.

"You appear to be well acquainted with the

subject," he said. "And this despite your claiming not to have read my work. I wonder whether you are testing me."

Alfredo groaned inwardly. Marsh had an expression of intense concentration on his face as if trying to force a reluctant bowel movement. His eyes had narrowed and the artificial grin seemed frozen on his features.

"I can't think why you should believe I might be testing you," Alfredo said.

"All that stuff you mentioned is the shop-front of the conspiracy. It's out there on the internet now anyway. Back in my day we had to join several dodgy secret societies, have a lot of group sex with some rough-looking crooks and tarts, and read a lot of boring, expensive, hard-to-obtain books in order to get even on the first rung of the ladder of true revelation. People these days have it too easy. "

"That's as may be. Anyway I'm not testing you. I haven't come as the representative of an esoteric order devoted to establishing a single world government. I don't belong to any conspiracy."

Marsh appeared disappointed. Alfredo suspected that he was somewhat looking forward to the possibility of being co-opted into the secret global elite after a short interview process. Moreover, the expression of extreme concentration on his face disappeared and he threw the remaining contents of his glass down in his throat in one go.

"Are you an atheist then? That's so dull. Everyone's an atheist nowadays. Except for all the Muslims of course."

"No, far from it. I'm a Roman Catholic."

"AHA! AHA! I knew it!"

"What do you mean?"

The Roman Catholic Church, Marsh believed, was one of the principal agencies working on behalf of the Magisteriarti. Some famous Russian author had explained it all in a chapter – that Marsh had photocopied – taken from a book written in 1880. The Church had chucked over the stuff about really following Christ (who was probably an ancient astronaut anyway) way back in 756 under Pope Stephen II.

"Well, it's like the Masons isn't it? Your regular church-goers are just like your regular lodge-goers. Dupes. Too far down the pecking order to know what's really going on right at the top. Orgies. Satan-worship. Exoteric and Esoteric aspects."

Marsh stared forlornly at his empty glass and then went on speaking.

"I suppose that it was Father Spencer who told you to try and get me to come along to church on Sundays? He's been at me ever since he came back. Keeps saying how Christian theology now depends on what the individual thinks about it from his own experience. Seems to me he's come around to my way of thinking!"

Alfredo was finding it extremely difficult to determine exactly what Marsh believed. He appeared to jump from one prior assumption to another, even if they were contradictory.

Alfredo went up to the bar and got some more drinks in.

"I hate Catholics," Marsh said once Alfredo had sat down. "No offence, because I was brought up one. Every week when I was young I'd see folk troop up to confession and every week the same folk were back confessing the same sins they'd promised not to do again. I'm not surprised they either chuck the whole thing in altogether or else don't bother going to confession any more. At least they're being honest about it. Anyway, I don't believe in sin. It's a stupid guilt complex. Freud showed that. I don't think there's anything worth worshipping in this world except sex, power and money, really. That's what all the Cardinals and the Pope are really interested in anyway. Always have been."

"Is that what you're interested in?" Alfredo said.

He found it rather distasteful that this leathery old man was still so obsessed with sex. Not that he was unusual. It appeared that almost all of this current baby-boomer generation of pensioners hated the idea of ageing. They acted and dressed as if they were eternal teenage rebels. Alfredo thought nostalgically back to 1981 (for him a mere yesterday) when the elderly had behaved – and dressed – with appropriate dignity and decorum.

"Look sunshine," Marsh replied, "you're probably still a virgin. Don't knock it until you've tried it. I don't worship anything. Certainly not a God who allows babies to die of cancer. Explain that one to me."

"I don't know that I can, but if there is no God then it's all absurd, both good and bad, and neither makes sense anyway."

"Absurd sounds the more likely to me of the two, compared to God."

"But if everything is absurd how could we recognise it as absurd? And if it is really all absurd, why is it that we even care about babies dying in agony?"

"That's just Jesuitical bollocks. Let me ask you this; why do you think your own religion is best?"

"That's obvious. I think the Gospel accounts are accurate. I think Christ really was who he said he was."

"Is it obvious? Maybe you'd have to have been there to know what happened. It seems to me that he could have been any number of things. I think it was his disciples who decided what he was, if he even existed, and they did so after the fact. You should read about the bloodline of the holy grail and what Jesus really got up to with Mary Magdalene."

"What's the grail got to do with it?"

Marsh chuckled throatily and took another gulp of his Jamesons and soda.

"That's another symbol. I've said before; exoteric and esoteric," he said.

"What do you yourself really believe?"

"I'll tell you in a minute. You know the old story about the cleverest man in the world?"

"It sounds familiar."

"A simple young monk goes on a pilgrimage to find and become a pupil of the cleverest man in the world who has reputedly studied all that is worth studying. This man lives alone in a vast cave filled with innumerable books of learning far out in a great desert. When the monk completes his trek, after weeks of travel on foot, he finds the cave and an ancient, raving hermit, filthy and with a long white beard. The old geezer has burnt all his books to keep himself warm at night. The monk asks him 'Are you really the cleverest man in the world?' and the hermit answers 'I certainly am! And you must be the most stupid! I've been expecting you!'"

The drink was affecting Marsh and he waxed eloquent.

"Look," he went on, "I get the whole idea that the

modern world is something of a fraud. I get the idea that there are unexamined assumptions about "progress" driving an ideology that most people have ceased to be aware of. Really I do. I even get the idea that you can't prove the validity, via the scientific method, of the materialist philosophy most atheists hold. But you Catholics are a worse alternative. You don't seem to recognise that even when people do admit that some of your criticisms are valid, they're also laughing behind your back at the way you've squandered your heritage."

"Knowledge doesn't die once it's been planted in the mind."

"No what happens is this. It becomes repressed. People return books of theology to the shelf, assume they've now taken all information into account, and then get on with living their lives, exactly as before. And those lives are lived in an age where society and any other books they read repudiate the conclusions reached in theology however much they were previously convinced on an abstract level. So they slip back to the comfort zones of popular culture and popular opinion that's being drummed into them all the time. And I tell you this; the idle layman who's bothered to read stuff like Thomas Aquinas or Henry Newman is every bit as unlikely to cross the threshold of a church as those who haven't bothered to read stuff like that at all. It's grist to their – ahem – philosophically – um – anarchistic mill. If it's intellectual chaos, which you may claim, at least it's their own individually chosen chaos. It's certainly a better informed chaos, for sure. That's all that I really believe in."

Alfredo was tempted to pull the argument back to first principles. He was tempted to use precisely the Thomist method of defining terms and proceeding on that basis, but he could scarcely see the point of it. If, thought Alfredo, a mind denies that reason is the basis of truth and then goes on to use reason itself to argue for that position, what is to be done?

"You know the funniest thing?" Marsh went on.

"No, but I'm sure you'll tell me."

"It's that – in the old days – I mean before the 1960s, it was the Catholic Church who dug its heels in, proclaimed "this is the true Church that Christ founded" and said the world must turn to its hard discipline if all mankind was to be saved. And what's happened since that claim was reversed at high speed? What's happened since it became so ecumenical, so "nice", so "tolerant", so "relevant"? It's become just as insignificant as any other of the endless number of modern Christian denominations. Now the Catholic pews are emptying out. The members of the congregation are dying off even as they shout out their damn Hosannas! Sure, the Pope gets some news coverage, but he gets it on the world's terms, and on its agenda, not his."

"You almost sound as if you miss the passing of the Catholic Church as it was."

"Not really. But at least it was a worthy opponent. This thing you've got nowadays is not the same. The likes of that lefty Father Spencer would be sitting here agreeing with me and banging on about how the Church now stands for life *before* death."

"I don't see why an individual can't resist and stand out against it all."

"AHA! Stand out against it all! That's a joke. How can you stand out against your own basic desires, the ones in your blood? All those hypocrite ascetics who run off to monasteries, all those celibate priests. They're the ones most burning with lust. Tears of remorse running down their cheeks even as they toss themselves off, night after night. Thinking about rogering nuns. Guilt complexes eating away at their sanity. That's not standing out. It's running away from natural impulses. At least since the 1960s we've had that Mary Whitehouse and Lord Longford sanctimonious crap on the run."

Alfredo pushed his own drink away from him. His eyes blazed defiance. But he remained silent.

"Look," Marsh went on, "I'm not trying to offend you. Just telling you how things really are."

He looked down again at his own empty glass. It

didn't seem as if Alfredo was now in the mood to carry on being generous and refilling it. In fact, he appeared to be disgusted by their conversation. It was time to push off.

"Well," Marsh said, "I've enjoyed our chat. But I've got to say goodbye. I've a date later with a still-up-for-it seventy-four year old Wicca lady I've been exchanging messages with on Tinder. Got to spruce myself up beforehand. Down below."

Alfredo remained silent.

"Look, to show there's no hard feelings I wish you'd take this as a peace offering. I feel bad about having upset you," Marsh said.

He rummaged around in his orange plastic carrier bag and pulled out a small glass bottle without a label containing 150ml of some pale green liquid with curled-up leaves resting at the bottom.

"What is it?" Alfredo finally said.

"*Artemisia Absinthium.* Home made from Old Bohemia. Secret recipe. The real deal. Wormwood leaves steeped in maximum alcohol. An occult connection of mine from Prague sends it to me. He's a huge fan of my writings and has translated them into Czech. He pays me in this stuff that he turns out. Go on, take it. I've got half a dozen more at my pad."

Alfredo paused uncertainly, but then slipped it into the pocket of his jacket. He thought he might take it along to the dinner party tomorrow at Doctor Huntley's as a conversation piece.

The two men parted rather awkwardly.

As he made his way home, Marsh drew the stares of several passers-by as he periodically chuckled out loud at his own wicked ingenuity.

One shot of that juice would give Alfredo the fiercest erection he'd ever had. The stuff, as well as containing the hallucinogenic wormwood, was also laced with a powerful, illegal, aphrodisiac.

As an aid to sex magic, Marsh had found it invaluable. Especially so at his time of life when the spirit is thrilling and the flesh is cheap.

CHAPTER TWELVE

IT was the night of the dinner party.

Doctor Isaac Huntley saw the thing as his great opportunity to establish a friendship, and, thus, a deeper sense of trust, with Alfredo. By observing him in a convivial and informal social gathering he could get at the human, personal, side of his nature that would be essential in his proposed best-seller book on the case. He mentioned none of this to Susan, however, since to do so would be to authenticate her claim that he was bringing his work home. Instead, he made sure he helped her in every possible way with preparations for the evening. He chopped the vegetables, went out and bought a selection of wines, and even consulted her on the appropriate background music. He had no idea that Meera Gupta had designs towards Alfredo of a very similar nature to his own, albeit in the much more immediate goal of obtaining a sensationalist inside scoop for B.B.C. Digital Radio 7 News.

As for Susan, she had little enthusiasm for the event. Her attitude was simply to get through it as quickly and painlessly as possible. To this end, she had started in on white wine spritzers two hours before. She realised Isaac was up to something, but since he had not specifically confided in her about Alfredo becoming the subject of a book he planned to write, she only had the vaguest notion as to his real motives. There was even a suspicion in her mind that Isaac had a secret thing for Meera, as did most of the men (even the celibate Father Spencer) that she knew. She was an exotic, feisty and independent modern woman. The virtues of the age seemed to be concentrated in her. Her brood of three girls had been acquired via a series of charming ex-lovers, all of whom were apparently wealthy, and who appeared to have been selected on the basis of not wishing to tie her down but to provide the best progeny. Moreover, Susan was desperately envious of Meera's offspring. They were delightful little children, quiet, always well-behaved, highly intelligent, and they apparently adored their mother. Really, they were little angels. Lovely.

Father Spencer was the first to arrive, and he turned up half an hour early.

Isaac opened the door to him and they exchanged handshakes with little enthusiasm. Isaac looked him up and down, registering raised eye-brows at the priest's jeans, cardigan and loafers. Combined with his bald head and Trotsky goatee, the man looked like a randy old college lecturer on a midnight spree.

"Haven't seen you in church lately, Isaac," Father Spencer said.

"Can't say I'm keen on listening to Bolshevism being preached from the pulpit – ahem – only joking of course," Isaac replied. He immediately regretted being so blunt, but the words were out before he could stop himself.

Father Spencer stiffened. He was reminded of someone he knew a long time ago, back in his early days when he was a history teacher. Hamilton was it? No, Hambleton. That was it. A dyed-in-the-wool Tory of the Keith Joseph type. Closet fascist.

"Come on in, Father, and get a lovely drink," Susan shouted from the inner depths of the Huntley sanctum. The slight slur in her raised voice betrayed that she had enjoyed quite a head start.

Father Spencer breezed past Isaac and wandered into the large kitchen. It was all pine, chromium and gleaming surfaces.

"Hello Susan," the priest said.

Mrs. Huntley was dressed in a figure-hugging,

strapless, small black dress and high heels. The dress was very tight and left little to the imagination. The colour of it perfectly matched her long, raven hair.

She was turning over salad with a vinaigrette dressing in a huge wooden bowl. She paused, took a few unsteady steps, and planted a kiss on the priest's cheek.

"Lovely to see you, lovely," she said. "What can I get you to drink? We have everything."

Father Spencer thought it over. A bottled beer to start, he decided.

"Do you have a bottle of Peroni?"

She nodded, went over to the fridge and bent down to get to the contents of the bottom shelf. Father Spencer's eyes widened.

Isaac, meanwhile, had appeared from the hallway just in time to see the priest's eyes almost popping out of his head.

"Get me one too, will you darling?" Isaac said, moving across to block off Father Spencer's direct view of his wife's rear.

"Ugh," she grunted, from the back of her throat, dismissively.

Ж

The next to arrive was Meera Gupta, who was punctual, to the very second.

Susan let her in and they air-kissed by way of greeting one another.

Meera realised too, with amusement, that Susan had been knocking back the booze for some time. Meera herself could (as she invariably put it) 'take-or-leave' alcohol and she prided herself on her oft-expressed life dictum that she personally didn't need to drink to enjoy herself. Although cocaine was a different matter.

Susan had actually made an effort and done herself up for the occasion, even wearing the classic "little black dress". Her lipstick was all wrong, of course, but only another woman would have noticed it.

"Wow. You look ten years younger," Meera said. "Well done, go girl!"

"Thanks," Susan replied, blushing through a hiccup. "Dinner's almost ready. Another ten minutes."

She was, however, suddenly discomforted by the sight of Meera's own outfit.

Her friend theatrically threw off her Aquascutum ladies raincoat to reveal skin-tight leather trousers, thigh length boots and a laced-up blood-red BDSM latex corset underneath. Meera stood there, with her hands on her hips, so that Susan could take it all in properly.

The strains of "Danse Macabre" filtered out from the living room, her idiot husband Isaac having just put the Saint-Saens symphony on the Bose system as background music.

As Meera sashayed into their presence Susan found it disgusting to witness how both Isaac and Father Spencer couldn't take their eyes off her, the two of them peering wide-eyed as they raised bottles of beer to their lips.

Meera sat down on the sofa, crossed her legs and began tapping away on her smartphone.

"Sorry guys," Meera said, "to be rude. But I want to check in with my mother. She's looking after my little girls and they get so upset if they don't hear from me. I said I'd send a few texts while I'm here."

"Please don't apologise," Isaac said.

"How thoughtful," said Father Spencer.

"Just need to check on the food," Susan said.

She wandered into the kitchen to sink another large white wine spritzer that was going to be five parts wine to one part soda.

Ж

At the same moment Freddie Sutton was having dinner in the Kettner's Pizza Express in Soho with his young blond Adonis.

"Freddie," said the latter, "your phone's making a fuss."

Freddie looked at the glowing screen, pressed an icon and read the following:

Operation Undercover has now commenced. Updates to follow.

"It's that damn Gupta woman. She's sending me text messages updating her progress on her so-called scoop."

He ordered two Sicilians from the hovering waiter and turned his phone off.

Oscar Wilde had brought his panthers here to dine, he thought, as he gazed fondly into the deep blue eyes of the young blond Adonis.

Although back in Wilde's day it wasn't a Pizza Express. Obviously.

Ж

Meera and Isaac kept exchanging anxious glances. Tension was in the air. Father Spencer couldn't work out why. It was as if they were in on some secret that they both knew about but that he didn't. The conversation was confined to perfunctory small talk, and the two of them kept looking over at the carriage clock on the mantelpiece above the open fire. It was all very odd. In the near distance the sounds of Susan rattling about the kitchen echoed. There was a pleasant aroma of something spicy drifting in from that direction.

Finally, Isaac broke the suspense.

"Our last guest is a little late in arriving," he said. "Still, I'm sure he'll be here soon. Probably held up."

"Can't you phone him, then? I mean – um – I am really keen to meet him," Meera said, rather curtly and with some degree of unwarranted impatience.

"Really, another guest? I had no idea," Father Spencer said, trying to keep his sense of annoyance out of his voice. "Who might that be?"

At that moment two events happened almost simultaneously.

The front doorbell rang loudly. A split second later, even more loudly, there was a huge crashing noise from the kitchen. The latter sound was followed by a shriek.

Everyone jumped up out of their seats.

"Can you check on Susan in the kitchen Father Spencer?" Isaac said. "I'd better open the front door."

Father Spencer was perplexed by Isaac's sense of priorities but hurried into the kitchen anyway.

Meera followed after Isaac as he went to the front door.

Ж

Alfredo had taken his time sauntering up the hill on the steep climb from Causton Road, via Peacock Lane, into

Highgate Village. He was not particularly looking forward to the evening but had promised to attend the dinner party and couldn't see a way to get out of it politely. He kept dawdling at corners, thinking over recent events, and bemoaning all the changes he saw in this new alien world of the future into which he had been thrust.

One of the most depressing, and stark, of the changes was that the old antiquarian bookshop on the hill had closed down for good. Only the front of the building remained, with its bow-window jutting out onto the pavement. Where once had been displayed piles of old books there was now the paraphernalia of a veterinary shop.

As he stood in front of it his thoughts went back to the times he had visited the emporium.

True, the owner had been surly. When Alfredo had first entered the man had shouted across the shelves that he hated schoolboys and didn't sell "bloody comic books". True, too, that he had been deaf as a post and that one could only communicate with him by standing next to him and almost shouting in his ear. But just as soon as Alfredo had mentioned his interest in Sinclair Egremont Xavier and his desire to obtain a complete collection of the Master's books, the owner had softened.

He, too, it seemed, was an Xavier devotee, and he

theatrically turned on the bank of light switches behind his desk, leading Alfredo into a short, locked corridor where there rested several rare volumes of the Master's published works all on a shelf in a neat row. They were not cheap, but Alfredo saved his pocket money, and, week by week, he purchased them one by one.

When this reserve stock was exhausted, the owner – just as soon as he acquired a new Xavier item Alfredo lacked – sent him a postcard with the price and details of the edition. Alfredo's visible excitement, as his Aunt Maria handed him the card from the post-rack in the hallway, was always delightful to her. At times she could not resist advancing him funds from his allowance expressly for the next purchase.

Alfredo finally turned away from the bow-window, forcing his thoughts back to the present, and crossed Highgate High Street in the direction of the house whose address Isaac had written down for him.

The place was easy enough to find, a large semi-detached house of faux-Gothic architecture, and he rang the front bell. There seemed to be some sort of commotion going on inside, but finally the door opened and he was confronted by the familiar sight of Doctor Huntley and, just behind him, looking over his shoulder, a smiling Asian woman who, for an unaccountable reason, was dressed up as a vaudeville stripper.

Ж

In the kitchen Father Spencer discovered Susan sitting down in front of the oven, looking thoroughly inebriated and distressed. The contents of a large casserole dish had been overturned. Some of it caked her black dress and legs, but most of it was scattered across the tiled floor like vomit.

"Ugh," she moaned.

"Let's get you up," Father Spencer said.

"Ruined, ruined, ruined," she went on.

He took her by the arm and helped her to stand. She perched unsteadily on a high stool next to the kitchen's wall-mounted pine table.

"Look. Burnt my wrist," she said. "Lovely."

She jumped off the stool and ran her wrist under the tap.

By now the others had wandered into the kitchen and were surveying the grim scene of culinary carnage.

Isaac didn't say anything, but simply retrieved a mop and bucket from the kitchen cupboard, with which he cleared up the mess.

"Well, it's not the end of the world," Meera said. "I know a lovely little Indonesian on Hampstead Lane that delivers. I'll find their website and we can look at their menu."

"I quite fancy Indonesian," Father Spencer said. He turned to Alfredo. "Didn't realise that you'd be here Alfredo. Quite a surprise."

"For me too," Alfredo replied.

Both looked unhappy at the turn of events.

Meera wandered into the hallway.

Before finding the restaurant website, Meera texted Freddie Sutton again with an update, a little annoyed that he hadn't bothered to reply yet.

"You'd better get some black coffee down you," Isaac finally said to Susan, as he rinsed out the bucket in the sink and turned on its waste disposal unit.

Susan ignored his suggestion.

She was staring at Alfredo, whom she'd not met before.

He was actually quite attractive in a boyish but still manly way, she thought.

"I'd better go and change," she said and disappeared upstairs, stopping only to tell Meera what she wanted from the restaurant.

As she did so, Isaac said in a quiet voice: "Bloody embarrassing. Sorry about all that. Susan doesn't really drink because, well, as you can see, when she does, she can't handle the stuff without making an exhibition of herself."

Meera wandered back into the kitchen and passed around the phone so that the others could look over the menu.

There was some hesitation from Alfredo, who was not at all familiar with the cuisine, but he seemed more at ease when advised that his choice consisted of a peanut-butter based dish.

"I'll pay for everyone, of course," Isaac said.

Meera dialled the restaurant number and handed her phone to him.

"Hullo," he said.

"Pengkalansusu Delight. What you want?"

"I'd like to place an order for a delivery, please."

"Very busy. Cyclist fall off bike. Much trouble."

"That's awkward. Look, I'll give you my order."

He detailed what they all wanted, gave his address and the voice said:

"You come here? Plenty room. Comfy."

"No, I want it delivered."

There was long pause and then a grunt.

"I tell you before. Cyclist fall off bike. Cut head. Very long delay."

"How long will it be?"

"One hour. Maybe more. Can't say definite."

In the background Isaac heard what sounded like a fist fight.

"We're only around the corner from you."

"Easy for you come here then. Do that. Very comfy."

"Look, I've already explained …"

"ALRIGHT! ALRIGHT! How you pay? Cash best."

"Fine."

"One hour. If lucky. Goodbye thanks."

Isaac handed the phone back to Meera.

"Are you sure about that place?" he said.

"Oh yes," she replied. "It may have the rudest staff in North London but their food is the best Far Eastern cuisine this side of Padangsidimpuan."

Eventually, they wandered into the living room.

There was some small talk, during which Isaac touched on the subject of Alfredo's medication and the necessity of his taking it regularly (during which Meera tapped away frantically on her phone).

The somewhat calmer atmosphere then prevailing was interrupted by a further scene in which Susan, still quite drunk, had decided to try and play Meera at what she thought was her own game. She wandered into the living room in nothing but black bra and panties before Isaac hauled her back upstairs again. This time, however, she decided it was best to have a quick forty winks and promptly fell fast asleep on the bed.

"Ruined," she murmured, before doing so.

Ж

The evening descended into chaos.

Both Isaac and Meera were almost subjecting Alfredo to an interrogation, one picking up where the other left off, but Alfredo was scarcely even responsive to their endless personal questions, and he murmured non-committal, vague replies. Father Spencer looked on with a mild sense of having been invited simply to make up the numbers. It was clear who was the focus of attention. They were, by now, all drinking wine (and on an empty stomach). Doubtless this was partially an attempt to loosen Alfredo's tongue, but rather than doing so it seemed to make him more reticent than ever.

After an hour and a half, when the food had still not arrived, Isaac phoned the restaurant again, but the line was engaged.

Then they had a row about politics. Meera started accusing Alfredo of being a fascist.

"I've noticed that most of the left appear to be Islamist sympathizers," he said. "Do you think it provides socialism with a soul?"

"What about the West's responsibility to the Syrian refugees?! And all the other countries it's bombed??" she blazed.

"Come on," Isaac said, in support of Alfredo's point, "Wives aren't allowed out of the home in most of the Middle East. They can't even worship together with men in the same room at the mosques over here."

"That's so racist," she replied. "It's your white

privilege talking. It's outrageous. All anyone decent wants is equality and fairness."

"Oh come off it," Isaac said. "What you really want is special treatment."

"Remember that Christianity has as bloody a martial history as Islam," chipped in Father Spencer. People in glass houses, etcetera …"

"I believe that there are many more Muslims here now than in 1981 and that it's the fastest growing religion in the West," Alfredo said.

"Yeh and terrorist Jihadi attacks are going on all over Europe," Isaac said.

"Actually," said Father Spencer, "it's Pentecostalism that's fastest growing. Worldwide anyway."

"Stop with the Eurabia crap! It's just a fascist conspiracy theory," Meera said – simultaneously – before looking down and tapping away again frantically on her smartphone.

She sent Freddie Sutton another message that read:

Fascist tendencies of Alfredo Salgado evidence of lasting brain damage.

"Well, my understanding is that Muslims used to regard Hindus and Buddhists as being more contemptible than Jews or Christians. The latter were 'People of the Book' but the former were regarded as Idolaters," Alfredo said.

"You're even having a go at my being Indian now!"

she said.

Freddie Sutton still hadn't replied to any of her text updates.

"Self-righteous outrage, even if loud enough, doesn't invalidate facts," Alfredo said.

"Don't accuse me of outrage, you dirty fascist!" Meera said.

"Yours isn't the Catholic way!" Father Spencer said. "The church has changed. The way you're looking at Muslims is the way people here in England used to look at us Catholics. You're a relic, Alfredo. As in the wrong now as you were then. You haven't changed a jot since you were my pupil. Talk about being stuck in the past."

"I can't say you've changed much either, Father," Alfredo said. "Despite your new vocation."

"These days the church seems more interested in being trendy and nice," Isaac said.

"Pardon me, but that's just a bourgeois slur," said Father Spencer.

The whole thing went around in circles, until the question of the food that had been ordered came up again.

Isaac phoned the restaurant for a second time, but the line continued to be engaged.

"Still can't get through," he said. "Perhaps we should order dinner from Pizza Express. They're quite quick."

Then he put on some Tangerine Dream music in the background.

Alfredo recalled that he had brought along the bottle of home-made absinthe that Dorian Marsh had given him.

"I brought something special with me," he said.

"I could really do with snorting charlie," Meera said. "Oops sorry, Father."

"Ha! Ha!" Father Spencer said.

Alfredo retrieved the bottle of absinthe from the pocket of his greatcoat, which was hung up on a peg in the hallway.

The others were, by now, not particularly concerned with what they were drinking. They were hungry, sullen and all conscious that the evening had not turned out to be to any of their own advantages. Only continued alcohol took the edge off of the worst of it.

Alfredo put the small bottle of green liquid on the glass coffee-table.

"What's that?" Father Spencer asked. "It's got no label."

"Bohemian absinthe. Imported. Pretty strong, I'm told," Alfredo said.

"There's not much of it," Meera said.

"Probably enough for one glass each," Isaac said.

He produced shot-glasses and they all knocked

back a single dose of the stuff.

Ж

It kicked into their bloodstream after fifteen minutes.

The hallucinogen-aphrodisiac in the spiked absinthe contra-acted, partially, with the drug that Alfredo was taking, and he was thrown temporarily into his cyclic fugue state. In addition, his legs seemed to be paralysed.

However, he was still the person most capable of resisting the sexual impulses the brew released from the depths, and was taken up entirely with the struggle against them. He leant back on the sofa and fumbled in his pocket for his last means of self-defence.

His eyes rolled up in their sockets. His teeth were clenched and he began muttering to himself through them, running the heavy black beads of his rosary through his fingers, reciting the *Pater Noster*, the *Ava Maria* and the *Gloria Patri*, decade after decade, unceasingly, in fierce concentration.

Sweat broke out on his forehead. He forced himself to visualize the Sorrowful Mysteries of Christ's Passion, the Agony, the Scourging, the Crown of Thorns, the Carrying of the Cross and the Crucifixion.

This act of spiritual warfare went on and on and he tried, through his recitations, to block out the other sounds of grunting, moaning and laughter that filled the room.

Occasionally eager hands grasped at him, but he fiercely pushed them away.

Once – and once only – he opened his eyes and saw the other three as they worked in and out of one another's flesh in blank-eyed, frenzied lust.

Ж

Freddie Sutton was in bed drinking cocoa with his blond Adonis when he finally decided to turn on his smartphone and check his evening messages before going to sleep.

He had a dozen texts from Meera. They became increasingly garbled and incoherent, and the final one contained a video attachment labelled "Here's a real scoop for you!".

He clicked on it out of idle curiosity.

At first he thought it was just some porno clip she'd attached by mistake, until he saw the sequence was actually shot on her phone.

Freddie's stomach turned and the warm cocoa repeated on him, tasting bitter and acrid the second time around.

CHAPTER THIRTEEN

ALFREDO had managed to shake off the worst effects of the Dorian Marsh brew and he gradually felt its influence fade. The fugue state subsided and time became linear again, instead of cyclical. It must have been a matter of two or three hours, objectively, before he was able to regain some measure of control over himself. He recalled stumbling out of the house just as the others were beginning to come to their senses, their bodies exhausted and drained, their minds in angry, confused turmoil, and he also recalled that Susan Huntley had appeared and begun screaming at them in shock and dismay.

He staggered back to the white house at Causton Road across urban landscapes of fallen terror, houses twisted by the dying effects of the hallucinogen, streetlamps like broken suns, and resolved to get out of the Highgate region for good as soon as possible. He couldn't bear the thought of seeing any of those people again, even via a chance encounter, and especially that devilish Dorian Marsh who was behind it all.

He collapsed in a heap on his bed at around three in the morning, and fell into a deep but anguished sleep, full of horrible dreams.

Ж

When Alfredo awoke it was just before noon, his body suffering from after-effects less fraught than those wreaked upon it by an alcoholic binge. His mind, however, seemed to have borne the real brunt of the damage. He kept having flashbacks, vivid and intense, and had to work hard to force the images from last night out of his consciousness.

He drank a lot of coffee and orange juice, consumed some cereal, and, in order to distract himself, logged into his email account.

There was only one message. It was from Ernest Quinn.

Dear Alfredo
Thanks for your email.
Glad to learn you're of the Household of the Faith!

I have not been involved with the nationalist-right for decades and repudiate their racial aims completely. It is a source of great regret to me that this past association has stuck in the consciousness of the public. But I digress.

I'm sorry to say that our having met one another back in 1981 is not something I can recall. It must have been very brief.

You ask about copies of my Sinclair Egremont Xavier biography. I do have a few of these left and would be glad to provide you with a signed one.

It occurs to me (in this connection) that you might be interested in attending a conference the society is holding in Brighton. We gather together tonight but the main events are tomorrow on Sunday. There is a special Mass planned in Xavier's honour that day too, it being his anniversary.

I realise that this is extremely short notice, but there is a single place still open, and if you emailed me before four o'clock today I could ask the hotel to keep the room available for you.

The full programme of events, details of the hotel, etc. can all be found at the link at the bottom of this email. Don't feel obliged to attend, since, again, I realise how short this notice is. But you would certainly have your copy of the book by the swiftest means, and you'd very much be made welcome at the event.

You'll find the other devotees of the Master's work an interesting, surprisingly varied, bunch! I must dash since, as you can imagine, I have a lot to get through today.

Thanks again.

Alfredo clicked on the link, found the hotel and programme details, jotted them down and finally rattled off a quick reply advising Quinn to please keep the room open for him as he would be catching the next available afternoon train to Brighton.

He went upstairs, threw some travel things in a portmanteau, swallowed two blue pills and departed immediately for the south coast.

Perhaps, he thought, he would at last find himself in the company of kindred, clean spirits.

Ж

Alfredo had, in the weeks since his recovery, confined his activities to the area around Highgate and was not prepared for the shock of the changes in central London. Everything was much cleaner, efficient and modern. The tube journey from Highgate had been the first surprise. Electronic dot-matrix boards on the platforms displayed the waiting time for the next train and its destination. Closed-circuit television cameras were everywhere. No one smoked any more down in the depths. There were no litter bins. No cigarette or chocolate vending machines. When the train arrived it was a gleaming new type of model that he'd never seen before. The conductor had, apparently, been removed. The carriages themselves were so pristine he thought first class compartments had been introduced. The adverts were as banal as ever, though there were subtle changes. Whereas previously they had been for physical products, like tobacco or alcohol, many were now for internet services or for social causes.

When he completed his journey and went above ground into central London he spotted that there were no mounds of litter piled up anywhere, no lurking white dog-turds to avoid, no rows of boarded-up shop windows covered in graffiti. Although most of the architectural features surrounding Victoria Station above street level remained intact, Alfredo had the eerie feeling that they could easily have been Hollywood sets, built for a futuristic movie. Despite the fact the signs and advertisements were still in English, fully half of the languages being spoken by the multitudes around him were the product of other cultures. He had no real sense of annoyance at this. He himself had been conscious that he was not quite English, being half Spanish, and the son of an immigrant – a reality brought home to him whilst he was a pupil at

Southwood School.

Yet it seemed to him that London had not so much gained a new diverse and multi-faceted identity, but rather lost all sense of its identity entirely. The English language was simply a *lingua franca* here now. London was a reference to a specific geographical site that contained a historical collection of buildings familiar from the past. It was a tourist attraction or a theme park. It could have been pulled down and rebuilt on the other side of the world.

On a huge television screen in the railway station a headline blazed the rolling headline message below scenes of black smoke rising over a cityscape:

Third suicide bombing in Europe in a week. Government urges public solidarity against any far-right extremist response.

People either talked into their phones, gazed at the screens, or listened to them via earpieces. It was as if the phones were actually controlling them, giving them impetus and coordination, as with a hive-mind. Female punks passed women in burqas, and men in Armani business suits brushed shoulders with hoodies.

Alfredo found a ticket office staffed by a person – not trusting the banks of machines that also dispensed tickets – paid his fare in cash (for a single ticket), and then wandered to the appropriate platform for the Brighton train through the hurried ranks of massed passengers as they weaved in and out of one another's paths balletically, while concentrating on their phones.

The train arrived after a few moments and he boarded it, as did an agitated crowd of other passengers who scrambled for the seats. For those unable or unwilling to force their way inside, there was standing room-only left.

The overground trains, much more so than the underground trains, had changed – almost beyond recognition. The iconic grey British Rail livery had been replaced with the livery of the privately owned successor serving this line. The old rolling stock, with which he was familiar, had gone. Manually-opened slam doors had been replaced by automatically operated pneumatic sliding doors. The windows were a sheer pane of glass running half the length of the carriage and couldn't be opened. The brave new transport was, Alfredo thought, like being inside a can of sardines on a factory production line.

As the train pulled away everyone again stared fixedly at their phones.

Ж

While Alfredo was travelling down to Brighton, the fallout from the events of the previous night reached a peak.

Freddie Sutton had called Meera into his office, confronted her with the video footage and they'd had a blazing row. For Sutton's part, he thought he now had the perfect excuse to sidestep entirely Meera's attempts to get onto his staff and bury the issue for good. He had not anticipated her line of defence. It was too audacious.

"I was set up," she said.

"By whom?" Sutton replied.

"The white Anglo-Saxon patriarchy."

"What do you mean?"

"Look, it's obvious. I was drugged and then forced to commit sexually degrading acts against my will."

"The other two engaged in the acts were also drugged, weren't they? The two men, that priest and the doctor?"

"So you're defending them, are you?"

"What do you mean?"

"I mean you're a man. You would say disgusting things like that. Misogynists always do. They obviously knew what was going to happen beforehand. They planned it. That's what men do. Exploit women. It's in their nature."

"But I'm gay for Christ's sake!"

"That doesn't mean you're not a misogynist. Often homos are. Though not lesbians obviously."

She had gone too far.

After they had shouted at one another for a few minutes more, Meera stormed out of Freddie's office and immediately began an online support campaign via Facebook, Twitter, Instagram and any other social media platform she could think of.

Her campaign outlined her drugging and sexual abuse by two representatives of the pillars of patriarchal power; the church and the medical profession. She insinuated that the B.B.C. was also directly involved and was trying to cover up the scandal.

An hour later she was 'trending' and had received tens of thousands of pledges of support.

Two hours after that she released a heavily edited version of the video footage on YouTube, containing a tearful introduction sequence explaining what had happened to her.

Pledges of solidarity shot up into the hundreds of thousands.

Freddie Sutton's blond Adonis furiously retaliated – on his own initiative – by anonymously uploading the unedited footage to a series of adult-only video websites.

Nevertheless, by the end of the day, the B.B.C. Governors decided to suspend Freddie Sutton indefinitely from his post, pending an investigation.

Meera tweeted in response to this that B.B.C. Digital Radio 7 News had long been institutionally misogynist.

Unfortunately the current spate of Islamic terrorist bombings distracted some of Meera's target Leftist constituency who followed B.B.C. Digital Radio 7. They were already fully occupied in explaining (on Twitter) that the true causal explanation and responsibility for the recent "so-called Islamist terrorist attacks" rested with the historical, hegemonic, imperialism of the whole U.S.A. industrial-military complex coupled with Republican Presidential candidate Donald Trump's vile rhetoric.

Moreover, the night before there had been, too, a very serious case reported on B.B.C. Digitial Radio 7 that also engaged their attention. A dozen potentially violent far-right extremists (under the 'pretence' of holding a candlelit vigil for those who had been killed) had needlessly provoked a group of a hundred peaceful, disco-dancing anti-fascists who had turned up to counter-protest.

The police had moved in swiftly to arrest all of the far-right extremists on suspicion of "an act of hate speech", but not before the hundred anti-fascists had bravely, *en masse*, managed to set fire to the offending banner bearing the slogan "Stop Avoiding The Issue" by using one of the right-wingers own candles.

An overexposed B.B.C. television and radio personality widely regarded as the most intelligent, nicest man alive – not to mention being a national treasure – and who was desperate to make up for a recent gaff he'd made about the homeless at an awards ceremony, expressed his sage opinions on the matter on a phone-in politics show just after transferring his lucrative payments for an afternoon's voice-over work to his bank account in Jersey.

Mickey Smart, the increasingly popular stand-up comedian, having heard the phone-in show, promised to do an emergency benefit gig at the King's Head in Crouch End over the weekend in solidarity with Meera Gupta in what he termed "a principled example of direct action and devastating satire levelled at fascists."

B.B.C. Digital Radio 8 Arts expressed an interest in covering it live.

Ж

"I want an annulment," Susan said. "I don't care how long it takes. I'll get one."

Isaac was sitting in the kitchen, hunched over a cup of coffee, with his head in his hands.

His career was ruined.

The sordid events of last night were public knowledge.

It was all over the internet.

He was a laughing stock.

Dodgy Doc and Pervy Priest enjoy a hot Indian Takeaway, ran the title of one link he'd been sent to a horrific website called "Men are Emperors" that had somehow got hold of the unedited footage.

The B.M.A. would hang him out to dry.

"Since we were married in church just a civil divorce is no good. I mean, obviously, we need one legally, so we'll get it, but it's an annulment I want," Susan carried on. "Our false marriage has to be unmade."

Isaac couldn't take in the enormity of the thing.

He had ruined his future.

No one to blame but himself.

"Obviously the fact you didn't want children indicated something fundamentally wrong in our marriage from the very start. I was blind not to see it. I tried to fool myself."

Tears welled up in Isaac's eyes. His upper lip started quivering. All his plans gone down the drain. No way back.

He snuffled loudly and wiped his snotty nose.

"I'm sorry for you."

Susan was still talking. She went on.

"You're just like a big baby."

No more prestigious medical conferences.

No more Highgate private clinic.

"But I want a real child. And I want a real husband and a real father for it."

No best-selling book about the Alfredo Salgado case.

His reputation was in tatters.

He was a "dodgy doc".

Probably even the N.H.S. wouldn't take him on.

"Isaac, are you listening to me?"

He looked up at Susan.

"What was that you were saying?" he asked.

It was the end.

Ж

In St. Jerome's it was Father 'Chuck' Driscoll to whom Father Spencer made his confession.

"Ah absolve yew in the name of tha Father an tha Son an tha Holy Spirit," Father Chuck said, while making the sign of the cross.

Outside the confessional box, Father Spencer knelt down and meditated on his penance.

Father Chuck didn't say a word, but wandered off somewhere.

Several minutes later, Father Spencer noticed Father Chuck was back, hanging around at the front of the church and glancing idly over the racks of Catholic

Truth Society pamphlets and then thumbing through one of them. The task appeared to provide an excuse for him to keep occupied until Father Spencer had finished his meditations and prayers.

"Seems like thangs have got outta hand," Father Chuck said. "Ah had this just naw."

He passed his smartphone to Father Spencer.

On it was an email text message sent to St. Jerome's inbox from a representative of the Archbishop of Westminster, informing Father Chuck that on no account was Father Spencer to serve the parish any further. The Cardinal's legislator advised Father Chuck, in no uncertain terms, that the machinery of the Ordinary was in motion and that his colleague was, until the process was complete, under an emergency penalty of suspension from exercising any of his priestly duties.

"Bad news travels fahst," Father Chuck said.

Father Spencer actually staggered a little, and clutched at the nearest pew for support.

"You didn't tell them, did you?" he asked the American, stunned.

"Ain't never broken tha seal of tha confessahnal, an nevah will. God help me so. C'mon, Den! Y'all don't know this thang from las' night is naw all over tha social media? Your – um – lady friend, Meera has made it into a scandal, an' make no mistake."

"It's the fault of bloody Alfredo Salgado and his spiked drink. He wants revenge on me. I've confessed my sins, will do the penance required. Tell the Cardinal's legislator …"

"That's true, ain't no denyin', an' cunfessun does yew credit," said Father Chuck, "but yew got Canon Law agin yew naw. Tha whole thang ain't so simple. Due process an' all. Yew gotta go befaw tha Ordinary. Ah reckon it's gonna mean a long trip to Afriky in tha end and years o' work in tha missions. Better un excumunikatin' yew tho."

"I didn't expect the bloody Spanish Inquisition. Not under this Pope."

Father Chuck, like most Americans of a certain age, was a huge fan of a certain British comedy, and took this as a humorous reference on Father Spencer's part and a sign that he was now taking it with a good and contrite heart. Almost without hesitation Father Chuck replied;

"No-one HEXPECTS tha Spanish Inquisition!!!"

Unfortunately, he only realised he had made a terrible error of judgment in trying to make light of the situation and cheer his fellow priest up when Father Spencer stormed off without a word.

Father Chuck never saw him again.

Ж

Meanwhile, as this was going on, Dorian Marsh was in the Woodman public house, taking advantage of their free wi-fi, and sipping at a half-pint of the cheapest ale. His eyes strayed occasionally to the door in the hope that someone he knew might enter and who he might tap for a loan or a drink.

He had finished browsing through the old comments on his blog and started looking at the latest results on Google search for unusual newsworthy events in Highgate. It was useful for him to keep on top of developments, just in case they had any bearing on his own occult activities and the opportunity to remind people about his local celebrity. It was a struggle to keep it from fading in the public consciousness. He had even occasionally shifted some copies of his pamphlets via this method.

Marsh saw a brand-new headline in the website of the *Highgate and Archway Bulletin* that had been posted online an hour before and was titled:

BBC AND BMA IMPLICATED IN HIGHGATE HIGH-JINKS

He clicked on the link and read all about the accusations made that afternoon by Meera Gupta. Since he didn't know her, or Doctor Huntley, it was only when he saw Father Dennis Spencer and Alfredo Salgado's names mentioned that he made the connection.

A broad grin spread over his horsey face as he read on.

So, the influence of his creeping Sex-Magick had not waned down the long years, and his True Will was still capable of causing chaos amongst the all-powerful Magisteriarti. Surely, he thought, the occult elite would be forced to note his mastery and come to an accommodation. It was well-known in certain circles online (at least where the adepts gathered to share the latest secret wisdom) that the Magisteriarti often paid off those who threatened to thwart their plans — and that they did so via the National Lottery. The numbers chosen by adepts were all logged. The idea that the winning numbers were generated randomly was a useful device to fleece the ignorant herd out of cash. If he bought a ticket for the next draw he now had a much improved chance of scooping the jackpot.

Thus far, he had only ever won ten pounds.

And that was two long years ago.

CHAPTER FOURTEEN

ALFREDO arrived in Brighton and detested the place. He had no way of comparing any changes made since 1981 – as this was his first visit – but he sensed at once that it was really a borough of London that happened to be situated on the south coast, with the overflow denizens of trendy Camden dumped into it.

He exited from the platforms onto the station forecourt, past a series of chain stores vying for the attention of bored travellers, then slumped down on a low wall, puffed on his electric-pipe, and consulted his written directions. The conference was to take place in a seafront establishment calling itself "The Hotel Grande Splendide".

Three homeless people came up to Alfredo, one after the other, asking for alms during this brief interlude, and he thereby rid himself of all his coins.

He set off down the sharp descent of Trafalgar Street, past a series of small shops or boutiques, which appeared to be designed to cater to bohemian college students and elderly hippies. It seemed the two groups prowling the area were almost completely interchangeable. The only things that distinguished them were the smooth skin and taut bodies of one type and the wrinkles and sagging flesh of the other. In speech, clothing, and manner, they were identical.

Eventually, Alfredo found himself wandering along the Grand Parade and passed by the Royal Pavilion, with its gaudy plaster minarets and domes, and its horrible attempt at eastern splendour.

The thing was infinitely depressing.

Nothing that was not artificial or fake could long exist in this region.

Though why the Sinclair Egremont Xavier Appreciation Society had chosen Brighton as the location for their conference was clear enough. Back in 1957, Xavier had written a novel called *The End of the West Pier* in which a disillusioned alcoholic writer returned to the Catholic Faith after years of having been lapsed. The final moment of crisis had come when the writer had considered committing suicide. During a six day binge he had decided to drown himself by jumping off the end of the West Pier at dawn, but experienced a religious re-awakening and eventually became an oblate instead.

It was not one of the Master's best books, but — *Return to Maidenhead Hall* aside — was his most popular with the reading public.

The sea came into view, or, rather, the English Channel did.

There was a sickly mist crawling across it, gradually making its way onshore.

Alfredo located the The Hotel Grande Splendide, which had undergone extensive refurbishment. The process was not, however, complete, and a wall of scaffolding obscured a large proportion of the mid-Victorian edifice. What could be seen of the outside structure was either whitewashed, or else plastered with stucco. It was difficult to tell. The thing had been badly bungled.

The staff inside the hotel were Polish. In one sense this pleased Alfredo, in much the same way as it would have done had they been Irish. He liked being amongst fellow Catholics. However, he found it hard to make himself properly understood.

He explained that he had a late reservation and was here for the Sinclair Egremont Xavier conference.

"Not Transhumanist?" The female Polish receptionist had said. She giggled.

"No," Alfredo replied.

She went away to consult with her Polish male colleague. They both looked at their smartphones and then he replaced her at the reception desk.

"Conference for scientists?" he said, smiling oddly.

"No, the writer's conference."

"Just two conferences here now. One is science, other is erotic. Adults only, I think. Yes that must be you. I keep up with the news. B.B.C. hi-jinks, huh? Wink, wink?"

"What?"

Alfredo had no idea what he was getting at.

"Sign for conference you want has gone up. Look."

The male Polish receptionist pointed across the room.

Alfredo spotted a large sign, with stick-on letters, positioned outside one of the bars and wandered over to it.

The thing read:

6.30 P.M. – S.E.X. CONFERENCE.

At that moment a person who Alfredo recognised as Ernest Quinn appeared. He came out of the bar holding a half-consumed pint of real ale. Spotting the sign he got the receptionist to put in the word "XAVIER" instead.

"Please, I told you: No use of that acronym!"

Alfredo wandered over and introduced himself.

Ж

Quinn had not changed considerably, in his appearance, since 1981. He was somewhat more thicker-set and his once closely shaven scalp now sported silver-grey hair. His accent had undergone a slight adjustment, but whether by conscious design or unconscious influence, it was not possible for Alfredo to tell. Certainly most of the sharp cockney edge to it had rubbed off. Quinn himself did not recall Alfredo, unsurprisingly, since their encounter had been so fleeting and had occurred over thirty years earlier.

The two were seated in the sea-view bar of the Hotel Grande Splendide, across from the other attendees at the Xavier Conference, who milled around either talking or pointing to smartphones, and who were obviously well-known to one another. From what snatches of conversation Alfredo overheard, they seemed to be anticipating the imminent arrival of someone very important. He received a handful of curious (even narrow-eyed) stares from the attendees, but attributed these to his being a stranger in their midst.

Quinn had passed over a signed copy of his Xavier biography to Alfredo as promised, and would not accept any payment.

"By the way, I'm afraid the special Mass for the Master has had to be cancelled," Quinn said, over his pint. "I'm sorry for it. But it would only have been you and me in attendance."

"Oh?" Alfredo replied.

"A strong objection at very short notice was raised by our Patron – and the Treasurer, the Secretary and the rest of the committee agreed with it. Even as Chairman I couldn't get the thing through."

"I don't understand, surely the Xavier Society would be highly pro-Catholic. There wasn't a more staunch defender of the Old Faith in English literature than the Master," said Alfredo.

"You'd certainly have thought so. I sometimes think they voted me in as Chairman simply to pay lip-service to the central Roman Catholic element in his work. Most of them weren't happy at all with my emphasis on his religion in my biography. They pretty much try and ignore it. The real driving force behind the society is the Master's son and heir, Victor Xavier. He's the Patron, you know, and bankrolls it. Runs the thing like a fiefdom."

"Surely he's a Catholic though? I remember reading – in Butler's memoir – that the son was training for the priesthood, right after he was sent down from Oxford."

"Lapsed straight after the Master died in 1970. Dropped right out of the seminary and opened a pub popular with stockbrokers in Amersham with his father's legacy. Hasn't been to Mass since. Hates the church. Actually he hates all mention of Christianity – Catholic or Protestant. Any religion, in fact. Even got quite keen on nihilism at one stage."

"That's awful, I can't believe it, the Master would have been outraged, and disowned him," Alfredo said.

It was a grievous blow. Alfredo had imagined that, if there remained one last bastion of traditionalist sanity in the modern world, it would be amongst the last remaining devotees of Sinclair Egremont Xavier. The disappointment was hard to bear.

"Heads up," said Quinn, "speak of the dev... erm, I mean – well, here Victor comes now."

A grotesque figure, in his late sixties, suddenly appeared in the bar. A figure from literary legend returned to life, and actually bowed, as if he were on stage taking a curtain call.

Alfredo blinked. Then blinked again. The vision clad in Harris tweed, plus-fours, and yellow golf shoes straightened up and swigged from a tumbler of whiskey and ice cubes.

The reality of this apparition made Alfredo almost gasp.

Memory made flesh.

The closest aspects of the son's physical resemblance to the father were astonishing – Victor Egremont Xavier had the same podgy, jowly features as the Master; the exact same highly florid complexion, squat, twisted nose and disdainful curl of the lip. The most notable differences were twofold; whereas the father had been only five foot five in height, the son was closer to six foot (the same height as his mother). And, whereas the father had been bald as a coot at the same age (and even resorted to donning an awful, ill-fitting wig), his son possessed a full head of natural white hair.

Victor Xavier gazed back coldly at the assembled group as all eyes expectantly turned to him. He was the centre of attention, and fully expected to be so. A ripple of applause ran around the gathering.

Having made his grand – solo – entrance, and received a measure of acclaim, he now seemed satisfied. He then turned his head and shouted over his shoulder in a booming, clipped accent:

"My lovely young wife!"

A young, shapely, raven-haired woman in her early twenties finally appeared. Presumably she had been waiting beyond the doorway. She tottered forward unsteadily into the bar on high heels, clutching a bottle of Bacardi rum.

"Who's that? His granddaughter?" Alfredo whispered.

"He's on his sixth marriage," Quinn replied, shaking his head ruefully. "Sharon. She was one of his barmaids, until last year."

"Shut yer big gob, sexist" Sharon said. "I'm 'ere ain't I?"

She suddenly looked over at Alfredo.

"Ere Vic," she screamed, "it's that bloke in the news wot was havin' a fit. That kinky fing wiv that Indian B.B.C. bird, y'know."

Ж

Shortly afterwards, Quinn and Alfredo were wandering slowly westwards along the King's Road that ran parallel to, but just above, the beachfront itself.

The late afternoon mist persisted as the sun descended towards the horizon.

The scene back in the hotel bar had finally alerted Alfredo to the reality that he was the object of unwanted, widespread public attention. Quinn had tactfully suggested that they get some fresh air and escape the immediate aftermath of Sharon Xavier's outburst. He had hoped to introduce Alfredo to a number of the other members of the society, but it was obvious the scene had made that awkward.

Some of them had even started (albeit surreptitiously) taking photos of Alfredo on their smartphones. The latest story about him being 'brain-damaged', and of 'doping his victims', was now being discussed in the wake of the monstrous events at Dr. Huntley's house the night before.

Once they were outside and clear of the hotel, Quinn led them in the direction of the West Pier.

"I expect you'll want to see one of the prime architectural landmarks of the Master's writings for yourself," Quinn had said.

Alfredo agreed, although he thought it would still be akin to the Palace Pier, but with a more elegant note. He was not at all prepared for the further shock that lay in wait, coming, as it did, almost immediately after the encounter with the Master's sole heir.

"There it is, you can vaguely see the outline," Quinn said, pointing beyond a construction site on the beachfront and an awful eye-sore of concrete and steel, like some brutalist shard, that was being newly erected.

Alfredo shuddered at another physical manifestation of the runaway philosophical juggernaut of 'progress'.

"That's the i-360 Tower," Quinn said. "Bloody awful thing that's going to be. A huge money-spinner for the council though, no doubt. Look, the West Pier's located just behind it."

Alfredo stared, but he couldn't quite make out the details because of the late afternoon mist. There was something there, but vague and gaunt, and it was hard to correlate the object with the idea of a Victorian pier – let alone with the paean of praise that Sinclair Xavier had lavished upon it in his classic novel.

The Master had called it, amongst many things, "the finest pier in Europe and the permanent envy of all its other coastlines."

They sat down on a bench and waited.

Finally, the mist cleared enough for Alfredo to be able to see properly into that middle distance.

The crimson light of the low, setting sun, off to the right of the structure, broke through almost all at once – the mist dissipated rapidly – and the rays illuminated the ghastly remains of the pier.

Only a central, titanic lattice-work of black metal loomed out of the water. The rest of it had collapsed or been burnt away.

The West Pier was skeletal and obscene.

It was dead, an eviscerated horror.

The red, backlit horizon seemed like blood, shed across the whole sky.

Alfredo had seen more than enough.

"I need to get drunk," he groaned to Quinn. "Very drunk. Perhaps even a six-day binge."

Quinn raised an eyebrow and replied:

"What the Master used to call a 'cocktail express to oblivion'?"

"That's the ticket."

Ж

Somehow, the Sinclair Egremont Xavier conference and the Transhumanist conference also being held at exactly the same time in the Hotel Grande Splendide, became mixed up into one big event. This was due, no doubt, in part to a lack of proper demarcation in the rooms and bars allocated to each, but was worsened, as the evening went on, by the fact that the delegates of both were drinking copiously.

Alfredo himself, upon returning to the hotel with Quinn, had at once started knocking back White Russians, to which drink Quinn introduced him. They were highly expensive, and he soon lost track of the amount he'd spent.

He was escorted out of the audience of a Transhumanist panel entitled "Human Biological Resources: the Impartial Case for Clone Farms" for starting a row during the Q&A session that followed it.

A paraplegic Transhumanist delegate in a motorised wheelchair had followed him down the corridor outside, screaming abuse directed at 'all the Elizabeth Anscombe type anti-scientific religious bigots trying to halt medical progress', whilst attempting to strike him with a rolled-up copy of *Wired* magazine.

Only a flight of stairs saved Alfredo from being crushed under the wheels of the vehicle.

If he thought he might find the Sinclair Xavier conference to be any the less controversial, Alfredo was mistaken.

He had wandered into a panel called "Sinclair Egremont Xavier Studies: The Way Forward in the 21st Century" and the opening remarks of the four panellists (a perfect gender balance in terms of representation), including Victor Xavier, stressed the need to celebrate the bohemian totality of the Master's work; and to acknowledge and fully apologise for elements of a 'problematic' nature in light of developments in contemporary culture. The word 'problematic' was a semiotic reflex that was repeated thereafter interminably by them in order to disavow and dismiss, without deeper consideration, a topic.

The thing went on for a hour. Alfredo could barely contain his frustration. When it came time for the Q&A session he leapt to his feet and gave vent to his feelings.

The patron of the society himself shouted Alfredo down from the stage when asked why no item on the programme of events made direct reference to the most important aspect bearing on a person's psychology; their professed religion. All four panellists had skirted the issue, except to criticise it in political terms.

There had been, Victor Xavier responded at the top

of his voice, far too much emphasis in the past on this one aspect of the writer's work. Critical theory now operated in a way that could liberate multiple interpretations that were far more productive than any narrow concentration on authorial intent.

"The Master – *your own father* – would have been ashamed of your attitude," Alfredo had said.

It was Quinn who had sorrowfully escorted him out of the conference room to the bar and began forcing black coffee on him as they sat in front of its long counter. A few delegates milled about, bleary-eyed and confused. They seemed like ghosts, material projections of the other-world, the world most important to them, contained in their smartphones.

"There's no point," Quinn said. "I tried putting this to the committee years ago. The so-called traditionalist Roman Catholic side of Xavier is an acute embarrassment to them. If you bring it out into the open in the hectoring way you did, all you do is get their backs up. They regard it as an eccentric pose or a kind of mental defect; even on Sinclair Egremont Xavier's own part."

"I'm astonished they haven't kicked you out yet."

"Again, some lingering respect for genuine diversity in opinion has saved me thus far, I suppose."

"Your 2002 biography of the Master, what sort of reviews did it get in the press when it came out?"

"Appalling. Nine out of ten were primarily interested in dredging up my past. The words 'written by a – or so he claims, former – fascist' in one form or another were utilised over and over again."

Quinn looked rueful. Then he went on:

"It came out at the same time as the film adaptation of *Return to Maidenhead Hall* directed by the media darling Benny Rivers who reimagined it solely as a bisexual farce set amongst the Bright Young Things of the 1920s. The adaptation gutted the Catholic elements except for the character of Father Shadwell – and he was turned into a comic turn; a stereotypical Irish priest drunkenly blundering in and out of the stately homes of recusant aristocrats. I suppose the only accurate thing about it was the depiction of Ladies Gertrude and Penelope Montague, the twin sisters who really did revel in causing chaos, and were disinherited for it. Anyway, it was a great success. Picked up a couple of BAFTAs. Made a packet at the box-office."

Alfredo said nothing.

He felt nauseous.

He looked down at the half-finished cup of black coffee.

When he stepped off the bar stool the distance to the floor seemed to lengthen inexplicably and he stumbled. All of his boyish insecurity rose up and he felt acutely, unendurably self-conscious.

Drink did him no good.

It was a torment when used as an escape from sorrow instead of an adjunct to joy.

It led to one final destination; remorse.

"It's time for me to disappear," he said.

"I've enjoyed our meeting," said Quinn. "And I'm sorry the event was so awful. God bless you."

Quinn and Alfredo shook hands and parted.

Ж

The following morning a gaggle of reporters turned up at the hotel looking for Alfredo.

They were not pleased to discover that their quarry had already checked out very early that same morning and they were reduced to hanging around the bar, seeking information from the delegates of both conferences that were being held in the Grande Splendide Hotel.

They obtained some useful newsworthy information concerning his disgraceful activities the night before, including a wilfully nasty, inappropriate diatribe levelled at a disabled delegate. To their disappointment, however, he did not seem to have repeated his Highgate activities, drugging anyone and then forcing them to engage in sordid, degrading sexual acts.

Ernest Quinn refused to have anything to do with the reporters.

Later that day, at the A.G.M. of the Sinclair Egremont Xavier Society, he was formally expelled for bringing the reputation of the Master into disrepute after being voted out as Chairman. The rest of the committee led the way in heaping opprobrium upon him for inviting along the notorious Alfredo Salgado.

The perishable cannot possess the imperishable.

CHAPTER FIFTEEN

ALFREDO Salgado had been walking west, on foot, for days. After leaving the Grande Splendide he visited a camping shop in Brighton, waiting until it opened, and there he had supplied himself with a backpack, walking boots, a full length water-proof jacket and slouch hat for the journey. He bought provisions along the way and had also taken the last of the blue pills.

At first he followed the coast, passing through Portsmouth, Bournemouth and Weymouth until, at Lyme Regis, he struck inland into country lanes, away from the population centres, crossing the Blackdown Hills. A few times he stopped at inns, ate ploughman's lunches washed down with ale, and wrote short notes detailing his progress on the journey.

There was no question of his returning to Highgate

and his aunt's house. Those days were over. There was no going back to the world. He felt compelled to make a final pilgrimage into unknown territory. A compulsion of the spirit was upon him. He would – he felt – know his destination only when he finally arrived there.

He knelt, twice a day, at the side pathways, took out his rosary and said five decades of prayers, whispering them to himself.

Once he came across an isolated village with a Catholic church and paused in his journey so that he could make a confession and hear Mass at the Saturday evening vigil.

A very elderly priest appeared from out of the sacristy, tottering along the aisle, passing the stations of the cross, making his way towards the confessional. He was lean and angular, his hair stark white, with only a little thinning at the crown. Although his eyes were rheumy and obscured by eye-glasses with thick lenses, and his face was now deeply riven with lines – radiating from the eyes and forming rows on his brow – Alfredo recognised him at once.

It was Father Nathaniel Laker.

Twenty years ago the priest had, after the destruction of the Pope St. Zosimus chapel, been sent away by Rome on a long sabbatical. When he returned home to England, after years in the missions in the far East, and also in Haiti, what he had experienced had made him come to terms with the idea that the survival of the Church in the whole world rests in its expression in a unity wider than one continent. Whereas previously he had regarded the Church as a European construct, now he had seen, for himself, that its truth resided in the God-incarnated message of hope and glory for all mankind. After his full reconciliation with Rome, the Church sent him to this distant parish in the west, where he served his small flock without any further occasion of scandal.

Alfredo knelt in the confessional, called to continual conversion to Christ in acknowledging his own fallen nature.

Father Laker received Alfredo's self-accusations with much astonishment – and not a little dread – and absolved him of his sins, conscious of the immense spiritual responsibility. For the priest had not heard such a scrupulous, searing, confession for many, many years.

He did not, however, recognise Alfredo, since his eyes were dim, the voice of the penitent was unfamiliar, and his own memory was marred by time. Alfredo, despite his wonder at encountering the priest, choose not to reveal his identity to his confessor.

And shortly afterwards the old priest – for some reason that he himself could not wholly account for – celebrated Mass that evening in the extraordinary form, relying on the old, dog-eared, missal from the Pontificate of Pius XII he had retained since his exile.

He was conscious of no defiance of Rome, no wilful disobedience on his part, only of an overwhelming certainty that the Latin Mass was, here and now, to be celebrated.

Even the table was set aside and he turned, as of old, to the altar, cleansing it with incense, with his back to the – at first startled – small congregation, making the sacrifice of Our Lord, instituted once only in eternity, dedicated by Our Redeemer at the Cross, repeated across the centuries. He chanted in Latin, the words coming back to him rapidly, despite long years of neglect, as in the accents of the Holy Saints carried across time, who, too, had celebrated Mass in the same tongue.

And the consecration –

Hoc est enim Corpus meum …
Hic est enim Calix Sánguinis mei …

At communion, the Faithful spontaneously knelt at the place where the altar rail had formerly stood, and received the Holy Sacraments of bread and wine, the flesh and blood of the Living God.

Later, shaking hands with the priest after Mass in the porch outside, Alfredo saw fear and wonder mingled in his eyes, as he contemplated this pilgrim stranger.

His congregation never spoke of the affair to outsiders, for it was their elderly priest's last Mass, and he passed away into glory later that very same night.

The last traces of the drug had now left Alfredo's body.

Ж

Alfredo carried on towards the west, his body unaccustomed to the rigours of a continuous trek, and he bandaged his blistered feet while resting on a path across Exmoor.

It was a relief to be free of the urban jungles where men and women massed together in lairs of concrete and steel, and huddled in sterile electric glows to ward off any reminder of the ancient night.

One evening a storm blew up, and Alfredo, rather than seeking shelter from it, ploughed on across the hills and troughs. He seemed to taste sea-salt in the rain-water, as if the downfall had been flavoured by its passage over the vast Atlantic ocean.

And in the voice of the storm, with its low rumble and murmur of thunder, came an apprehension of the sacred – a recognition that God had first revealed himself to men through the cycles in nature, and the mysteries of life and death and eternity, which only they, in all creation, could discern.

The storm finally passed, the last of its clouds trailing off to the east, and the sky cleared, the inky blackness dotted with thousands upon thousands of stars. Alfredo thought of their immensity, the distance between them, and tried to work his thoughts across the gulfs of space, as far as he could imagine, to all measurable distances short of infinity. No scale is stupefying in itself without humankind to realise it, and nothing could surpass the Absolute Mystery. Yet – when one poured one's prayers into the unknown – when that leap of faith was made – there came the conviction that they were not uttered in vain but were heard. For in the final reckoning all prayers are petitions that His Will be done, even when uttered in agony by the Incarnation of the Absolute Mystery upon the cross.

It is not to be thought that Alfredo vainly regarded himself as a prophet cast out into the wilderness. He knew, rather, that each and every man – in the end – must face his own apocalypse, and that his individual time of reckoning had come. Nor did he see himself as a martyr. That honour he was not worthy to achieve.

He sat down amidst a clump of rocks, the great bulk of Dunkery Beacon rising in the distance to the north. He lit a tea-light candle, nestled it in a hollow, and behind it, placed his wooden locket which, when opened, revealed Icons of Our Lord and Our Lady. He crossed himself, and went through his devotions on his knees, rolling the rosary through his numbed fingers.

Afterwards he laid out a handkerchief, consumed the bread contained therein, and fell, exhausted, into a deep sleep.

Ж

When he awoke the next day, he realised that time itself was closing in on him once more. He could not remember how he had reached the place where he had awoken. And his last memory was of the Mass in the Catholic church, which to him seemed like yesterday. He had – against this eventuality – kept up the record of his journey in a small notebook, and it was only by referring to this he realised what was happening to him again. It was not unexpected, of course, but the necessity of reaching his goal before his condition rendered it physically impossible was now doubly urgent.

He ate a breakfast of oats mixed with dried fruit, washed down with bottled water, and then pressed on in his journey. Occasionally he consulted his pocket compass, to ensure that his direction west was constant, and before long found himself compelled to enter into a thick wooded valley, keeping to a narrow path of red-brown dirt. As he progressed he watched the sunlight dance in the leaves and the branches overhead, and he listened to the murmur of the trees, shrubs and bushes, as the breeze gave them a voice.

Occasionally he encountered other people, mostly dog-walkers, but when they saw Alfredo their brisk "good mornings" or "good afternoons" were stifled. The animals pulled at their leads in order to get closer to him, but the strange ecstatic look they saw in his eyes made them draw back, and made their owners worry that Alfredo was some kind of wandering, possibly dangerous, lunatic. Moreover, he had been wearing and sleeping in the same clothes for days now, and it was only towards evening that he found a bubbling stream of clear running water, where he cleansed himself. Then he scribbled down an account of the day's journey as the twilight took hold.

He sat there in his damp garments, drying them by the warmth in his own body, and the shadows around him deepened, finally giving way to darkness. The woodland valley murmured to itself in the stillness of the night, its chorus more sharp to human ears than it was during the day.

Alfredo set up his little shrine, made his devotions by candlelight, and then experienced another fugue.

Ж

He thought, at first, he had awoken from sleep. But when he realised it was night and that he felt none of the sensations of moving from unconsciousness to consciousness the process of awakening engenders, he next suspected he had suffered another attack. At once his mind tried to work back to his last memory – that of leaving the Mass, once the holy ritual was complete. He was convinced that it had been a very short time ago, probably less than an hour. Everything in-between was a blank. Why were his bandaged feet worked raw as if by miles and miles of walking when he had only come such a short distance?

He fumbled for his notebook, leaning down on the scrubby grass, close to the light of the tea-light candle. The last entry, which of course he had no recollection of writing, detailed the missing hours. The cycle of interior time was turning a shorter curve, and would continue to do so. Alfredo could not yet determine at what rate it would shorten, but the ultimate, and terrible, end appeared certain. It would eventually result in a repeat of the fifteen minute sequence he had suffered for those lost, blank thirty years of his life.

Alfredo had known all along, when he set out on his pilgrimage, that death would be its likely consequence, but he had not yet reached – he was certain – the appointed place for the final rendezvous.

Some inner, inextinguishable, conviction told him so.

All he could do was to drive himself harder.

Time had revealed itself again as his foe.

He gathered up his meagre belongings and walked into the night, turning over, in his concentrated thoughts, a list of the names of all the Holy Saints that he could recall from their liturgical feast-days, and pleading for their intercession on his behalf — interspersed particularly with pleas to the Blessed Virgin.

Ж

He had walked during all of the night, though close to exhaustion, and had left behind the wooded valley. His trek now was over rising and falling moorlands, with the sea always to the north, just over the line of hills far off in the distance. Insomniac disorder fragmented most of his thoughts.

Gulls circled overhead, venturing inland in search of food, and were it not for their angry cries, Alfredo might have mistaken them for angels. They clustered and wheeled in the purplish-red dawn sky at his back, as if dancing in the light of the rising sun.

Later, at noon, Alfredo briefly stopped at an inn, but was refused service. Outside he was told by a bloated farmer, far into his cups, that there was talk abroad of a group of Romany travellers being in the area who would infiltrate a pub one at a time – sending in the eldest first – in order to drink all day and cause violent chaos later on – as their kind did. It would have been sinful to go back to complain and explain the situation. Alfredo preferred to have been turned away from such a place than to have quenched his thirst and assuaged his hunger there.

And, several miles further on, he came across a run-down caravan, half-hidden in a field, where a family of six lived, who freely gave him bread and wine. They amused themselves with guitars and dance and, for a few hours, he shared their hospitality. And when they asked about him, he told them of his pilgrimage. They did not seem surprised.

"There is a place," said the mother, "across the way. Another five miles walk to the west. What's left of an old abbey. Perhaps that is it."

She wrote down the route, and formed a crude map, on a scrap of paper and pressed it into his hands.

When, finally, he departed, with many thanks, Alfredo left all the remaining money he had between the pages of one of the children's well-thumbed and battered copy of a Gustave Doré illustrated *Scenes from the Bible*.

Ж

He reached the site before another mnemonic fugue could blot out the recollection of the encounter.

Without the directions he had been given he did not see how he would have found it. There were no signposts to the destination, and it was so far away from any existing village, or the paths of tourists, that a wanderer in the wilderness could only have stumbled across it through sheer chance.

He had taken an unmarked path through a dense forest, and the way forward was far from clear. Fallen logs, branches, and treacherous, exposed tree roots, clogged the route. Brambles tore at his legs, drove thorns into exposed flesh, and the snaking waywardness of the narrow passage through the obstacles seemed designed to madden the person who followed it. Quite how even his friends the travellers had discovered its location was a great mystery.

He bandaged the fresh wounds on his hands and legs, and attended to those older ones on his feet – now a mass of blisters – and pressed on.

Finally at dusk, he came to a small clearing, surrounded on all sides by the forest, and arrived at what remained of the abbey.

Doubtless some record of the site existed, as with other former abbeys, but its ruin and neglect was such that it bore no modern relation to the likes of a Tintern or a Malmesbury, which are thronged – at least since the Romantic era – by curious visitors in search of the Gothic sublime and the picturesque.

There were some few sections of the medieval abbey church still standing. Part of an exterior wall in what must have been the nave, with two peaked arch windows and a buttress. An isolated supporting twenty-feet high central aisle column stood a way behind it, broken and weathered. At a further distance the remains of a south transept could be determined by the low running walls at waist height. All of these structures were overrun with tenacious ivy, including that portion of the abbey church of which most remained; two walls of the Lady Chapel. These were not wholly intact, although the four peaked arch windows in one of them, some outside buttresses, and a low doorway in the other, had outlasted the initial depredations of the venal Henrician dissolution and the subsequent ravages, down the centuries, of both vandalism and the elements of nature. Of the various other out-buildings associated with an abbey – cloisters, cellarium, chapter house, for example – there appeared no above-ground trace.

Alfredo crossed himself as he entered what was left of the Lady Chapel and threw off his heavy pack. He got to his knees and began to pray the rosary before the little shrine he erected there, in marvel at God's grace and in thanks for the blessed intercession of the Holy Virgin Mother of Our Lord and the Saints. For Alfredo knew that his pilgrimage was at an end.

Ж

Days passed. The cycle of interior time within Alfredo rapidly returned to the fifteen minutes duration that had once been normal with him, before Dr. Huntley's therapeutic drug treatment. The running account he kept in his notebook became meaningless; a series of confused, jumbled, repetitive lines hastily scrawled as if by an ague-ridden hand. Sometimes it was dawn, sometimes dusk, sometimes day, sometimes night. Often he was hungry, often thirsty, for his reserves of food and water were almost exhausted. On several occasions he had soiled himself, and he now reeked of excrement and urine. Insects infested his clothes, feeding off him.

And then the cycle of interior time narrowed even further.

Fifteen minutes became ten, then five, then one.

And still it went on.

Ж

Father Dennis Spencer emerged into the clearing and heard the strangled cries coming from the ruined Lady Chapel.

He had followed Alfredo's progress across the West Country, after having learnt his enemy had been in Brighton at the Sinclair Xavier conference. As ever, Alfredo had left scandal and disgrace in his wake. Father Spencer trailed him over the country, always a week behind, even occasionally losing track of his quarry. Once he had reached the little village, in mourning for the recent death of Father Laker, he suspected that Alfredo would not elude him. The connections were coming together. Nevertheless, had he not encountered the gypsy family shortly afterwards, who, upon learning he was a priest, told him all about Alfredo and his pilgrimage towards the lost abbey hidden deep in the wilds, Father Spencer might have been thwarted at the last.

And from that point on, it was only a matter of when – not if – he would locate Alfredo.

The car accident back in 1981 should have been the end of it. Father Spencer had had that on his conscience for decades, though he told himself over and over again it had been an accident and he had not intended, deliberately, to run the boy down. Surely his past sins had been washed away at the baptism that signified his new spiritual life? Moreover, he had even entered the Catholic priesthood, adopting the faith of the very person he had wronged. Hadn't he done a full and proper penance since then, serving the weak and defenceless for years in one of the poorest parts of Latin America?

And then the boy had come back, almost from the dead, decades later, as if to haunt him, and had wilfully destroyed his standing with the Church, wrecking his life all over again.

Ж

Nothing, however, could have prepared Spencer for what he found. Alfredo was curled up in a ball on the grass inside the ruined Lady Chapel.

He was filthy, stinking, wallowing in his own filth, and he moaned to himself in a cracked dry voice that was no more than a whisper. His body spasmed continuously, and flecks of foam bubbled at the corners of his mouth, as if he were suffering a continual epileptic fit. His eyes were wild, deranged, darting in one direction and then in another, over and over.

There was surely only insanity left in that dying shell. Nothing could save Alfredo now. Death was imminent. There wasn't even enough time to get him to the nearest doctor or hospital.

The thing could scarcely be regarded as human anyway. Spencer had to fight down the wave of revulsion that swept over him. It would be an act of mercy – as with any dumb animal in pain – to smash its brains in and grant it immediate release from its suffering.

His gaze fell upon a chunk of heavy stone that would serve the purpose.

Then he turned back to the human wreckage.

He recalled his penance, found himself kneeling beside Alfredo, cradling him in his arms, making the sign of the cross on his forehead, and murmuring the words of the Last Rites. He pressed water to his mouth, wiped away his tears, and sat and prayed until – not long afterwards – Alfredo departed this life and finally triumphed over Time.

ABOUT THE AUTHOR

Mark Samuels is the author of five short story collections; *The White Hands and Other Weird Tales* (Tartarus Press 2003), *Black Altars* (Rainfall Books 2003), *Glyphotech & Other Macabre Processes* (PS Publishing 2008), *The Man who Collected Machen & Other Stories* (Chomu Press 2011) and *Written In Darkness* (Egaeus Press 2014). He is also the author of the novel *The Face of Twilight* (PS Publishing 2006). His tales have appeared in many prestigious anthologies on both sides of the Atlantic including *The Mammoth Book of Best New Horror*, *Year's Best Fantasy and Horror*, *The Weird*, and *A Mountain Walks*. Forthcoming books by him include a new collection of strange stories, *The Prozess Revelations.*

50079859R00194

Made in the USA
Middletown, DE
26 October 2017